Stereo Sanctity

By
Mike E. Purfield

PublishAmerica
Baltimore

First printing

ISBN: 1-59286-123-7
PUBLISHED BY PUBLISHAMERICA BOOK PUBLISHERS
www.publishamerica.com
Baltimore

Printed in the United States of America

For Neen and the perfect little grip she has.

I

A Hell of a Message from Hell Today (1985)

At 256 Tunisia Avenue, Tanya Shields woke up on her bed. The television flickered light in the room and tricked her into thinking there was a lightning storm. Realizing there was no storm, she reached over for the remote in Danny's hand.

Danny wasn't there.

She heard a hyperactive banging from the hall.

Worried, Tanya left the bed. She slipped on her ducky robe and covered her slim 31-year-old body. On bare feet, she walked into the hall. She passed Freddie's bedroom and peaked inside. He slept with his Transformer sheets tangled around his limbs; his face concentrated on a dream. Tanya closed the door and tapered the sound to Freddie's ears.

In the living room, Tanya found Danny at the front door. He nailed planks of wood across the threshold; a toolbox opened at his bare feet. Sweat soaked through his T-shirt and pajama bottom.

Tanya stepped closer to her husband but kept a safe distance from his hammer. "Danny?" she said.

Danny stopped hammering and twisted around. His fear-filled eyes stared at Tanya. She knew that he wasn't seeing her. Danny walked over to Tanya, raising the hammer for protection.

Tanya moved out of his way.

Danny stepped past her and looked around the living room. He checked the couch, the fireplace, and the tiniest spots behind the furniture. He walked into the kitchen and looked inside the dishwasher.

With nothing left to check, but still cautious, Danny walked back to the door. He picked up another plank of wood and nailed it up.

Tanya knew not to wake him. This wasn't the first time Danny had done something like this. A few nights ago he changed all the locks in the house. Then, a few weeks ago, he attached army-style booby traps on the doors. If someone broke in, the intruder would set off a sledgehammer aimed for the head.

On the way back to her room, Tanya found Freddie at his bedroom door. His sleep-crusted eyes curiously looked at her.

"Freddie, what are you doing?" Tanya asked.

"What's that noise?"

She kneeled down, blocking the 10-year-old boy's view into the other room. "Oh, Daddy is just working on something."

"Now?"

Tanya smiled at his amazement.

"Yeah, I know and he knows," she said. "But you know how your father gets when he sets his mind to things. Try and go back to sleep."

"Okay."

Freddie kissed her cheek and went back to bed. Tanya closed the door and walked to her own room. She dropped her robe on the foot of the bed, covered herself up with the blanket to her chin, and watched the open bedroom door.

The hammering stopped after a half hour, but Danny didn't come back to bed. Tanya relaxed enough to close her eyes and fall asleep. She woke up later when she felt Danny's body slip into the bed. Tanya carefully looked at him. Danny was asleep.

* * *

Tanya and her mother, Melissa Deal, moved to Owel from Asbury Park, N.J. when Tanya was seventeen years old. Her father, Keith Deal, died five months prior. His heart failed at the bank where he worked. Keith stood at the door in his security guard uniform when he felt a pain in the left side of his body. The paramedics didn't bring him back. Keith Deal was D.O.A.

Melissa was dependent on Keith. He was the money-gatherer of the family. Melissa had a few part-time jobs but they never lasted long. She could not perform menial jobs like cleaning up or unpacking boxes.

Whenever Melissa gave the boss a hard time, they told her to get an office job if she didn't want to do this one. Melissa couldn't find an office job due to her lack of skills. She tried to accomplish what they expected of her, but she ended up ashamed and debased. Melissa quit the job before she finished the task.

Back at home Tanya did everything that her mother was too superior to do. Since she was eleven years old, Tanya cleaned the house and cooked the meals. Tanya didn't mind doing it. She convinced herself that her mother had a mental problem and a fear of lower-class domestic life. Tanya wanted to help her father with whom she had a strong connection. Tanya knew Keith busted his ass, working over-time to make up for the unemployment Melissa went through. Tanya wanted life easier for him. Keith saw Tanya's hard work and often showed his appreciation with a few dollars and small gifts.

When Keith died, Melissa fell apart, worrying about who was going to take care of her. Just two weeks after the funereal, Melissa started to date a few men and assessed them for marriage. The dating disgusted Tanya, but she wasn't too surprised. She knew Melissa had no pure love for Keith.

While Melissa hunted for a husband, Tanya noticed the mortgage, the money accounts, and the bills. The money Keith left them was decreasing. Instead of paying bills, Melissa used it for more important things: new dresses, make-up, etc. They had to move into a cheaper home. Tanya found an apartment at the edge of Owel, just on the border of Jackson. It was the top half of a two family Victorian house.

At first, Melissa didn't want to go. Tanya then sat her down and showed her the bills and the money left in their account. Tanya told her mother they would be kicked out and homeless if they didn't pay the bills. Melissa's mind shifted in favor of the move. How could she meet a man if she was homeless?

Tanya started school at Owel High School that September. She also worked 30 hours a week at the local K.F.C. Tanya worked every night and took over-time as much as the manager allowed. She came home, tired and greasy, and did her homework. Her day ended at 1

A.M., then started again at 6 A.M.

Melissa found a job as a hostess at a local restaurant. She loved it. Melissa dressed up everyday, and felt superior to the staff. All she had to do was show the customers to their tables. If there was a mess, someone else cleaned it. Plus, Melissa met a lot of rich men.

As for Tanya, life felt hard with no reward. All she did was work and go to school. She had a few friends, but she was too tired to see them. Tanya felt like her father when he came home at night. No one was there to appreciate her, only to take what she earned. Melissa did nothing to help except give Tanya part of her paycheck for the rent and food. Tanya took care of the finances and cleaned up the apartment so Melissa could bring a possible husband home to entertain.

Then a little light came into her life.

In late October, she fell asleep with her face in her open Algebra book in study hall. A boy with an arm cast sat next to her. He told her that she was snoring and drooling on the pages of her book. Completely embarrassed, Tanya dried her face and book.

"Don't you get enough sleep?" the casted-boy asked.

"No. Not really," Tanya admitted. "What happened to your arm?"

The boy turned and took away the smile Tanya thought was so cute. "I hurt it one night."

"In a fight?"

"No. Accident."

"Oh."

"My name is Danny Shields."

"Tanya Deal."

* * *

The alarm played the morning news at 6 A.M. Tanya lowered the volume to a tolerable level. She turned to Danny and watched him sleep.

Although they were the same age, Danny looked a lot older. His temples grayed up on his light brown hair; lines formed around his eyes and mouth. They didn't look like smile lines, quite the opposite. But underneath all the hard changes, Tanya still saw the same smiling face that protected her since the first day they met; before life turned scary.

Tanya smiled down at Danny. She placed her palm on his chest, under his shirt, and made circular motions. He opened his eyes and smiled back at her. They both knew that they were going to delay their day. The morning was the best time for them. At night they were both exhausted. Plus, Danny had the stench of garbage he brought home from work. He drove a truck for Plutarch Waste Management in Staten Island.

"Ooo, you're cute," he said. "What's your name?"

Tanya straddled his hips and rubbed his belly. "Does it matter," she said. Tanya lowered her mouth to his.

"Just want to know what name to call out when I cum."

"What makes you think your mouth won't be busy doing something else," she countered.

They both smiled at each other and got down to business.

* * *

Tanya ate breakfast with Freddie in the kitchen. They were dressed for the day. Freddie worked on a bowl of Lucky Charms, picking out the marshmallows and eating them. Tanya looked from her eggs and toast at Freddie and gave him a suspicious look.

"I hope you're going to have more than marshmallows for breakfast," she said.

Freddie took the spoon, scooped up the healthy bits and mouthed it, chewing loudly and smiling.

Tanya smiled back. "Thank you."

Danny entered the room and kissed Tanya and Freddie on the top of their heads. "'Morning all." He then looked into the living room and noticed the boarded front door. Danny walked over to the barricade, confused.

Tanya stepped up behind him.

"Did I do this?" Danny asked her.

"Last night."

Danny looked at Tanya. "I don't know how... I'm sorry."

"It's okay. We'll just use the back door."

"I'll fix it tonight. I promise."

"Okay."

"I'd do it now, but I'm running a little late this morning."

"Oh, what have you been doing?" Tanya prodded.

"Not with the boy in the room."

"I can hear you," Freddie offered from the table.

"See," Danny pointed out.

Back at the kitchen, Tanya cooked Danny an egg sandwich for the road. Danny gave Freddie a kiss on the top of his head and made plans with him to help take the planks off the door. Freddie looked forward to it.

Outside the house, Danny kissed Tanya good-bye.

"I love you," she said.

"I love you more," he smiled back.

* * *

Tanya knew Danny was a sleepwalker since they started dating in high school; it never bothered her. She discovered it herself the first time they slept together while her mom was away on a romantic weekend. Tanya woke up and found Danny roaming the apartment, following something, playing a game that only he could see. When Tanya confronted him the next morning, Danny had no idea what she was talking about. Danny never knew that he was a sleepwalker.

At home, Danny lived with his younger brother by two years, Ray, and his mother, Juliana Shields. Danny's father, Bernard, died four years ago from a self-inflicted gunshot wound to the head. Bernard was a sleepwalker all his life. In fact, Danny believed that his father was asleep when he shot himself.

When Tanya broke the news to Danny about his own late night strolls, he worried. Danny started tying himself with a thick rope between the leg of the bed and his own leg. It worked. In the mornings, Danny found himself on the floor and attached to the bed.

Then there were the Beings.

Danny had seen them since he was a little boy. He told Tanya about the first time. Danny slept in his bed, and they floated over his body. At first, he was a little frightened, but then he grew used to them, and realized that they didn't really do much. They watched and smiled. Then the Beings became a little daring. They touched Danny, tickled him or played games with him.

When Tanya asked Danny what they looked like, he drew her a picture. Most of their features were human. They had arms, legs, and a head, but their skin was waxy and white. Their faces were perfectly round and flat with cat-like noses and slotted eyes that revealed green and milky light. Their mouths were vagina-like, horizontal.

Tanya accepted the Beings. Yes, it was weird but she found them non-threatening. Danny was the sweetest person she had ever met. She considered herself luckier than the rest of her friends at school who had to deal with pussy hungry boys that never gave them the time-of-day unless they spread their legs or opened their mouths for six inches. Danny never rushed her. He always thought about her and how she felt. Danny never dragged her anywhere, but asked her what she wanted to do. When Danny asked her to marry him that summer after graduation, even though he was a hallucinating sleepwalker, Tanya said, "yes" before he could finish the question.

* * *

Tanya sat in the break room and ate a burrito and diet soda from the Jamesmart snack bar. Charley Blair, a man in his mid-twenties who worked in the automotive section; and Kim Lit, thirty-six and head cashier, sat across from her. Kim endlessly chatted about a movie she saw the other night called "Sixteen Candles." Tanya zoned out, more interested in how Kim talked and ate without taking a breath.

A half hour later, Tanya finished her food and left the room at the point where Kim declared her sexual attraction to Anthony Michael Hall. Tanya walked out into the store and slipped on her blue apron where plastic tags advertised her name and the 40% off sale in her department.

Tanya worked in House Wares for the last 5 years. She liked it, but she didn't love it. It was a job. She was around long enough to be one of the highest paid employees. Plus, she had great benefits that covered Danny and Freddie, making the sick times easier on them, especially Freddie.

Even before Freddie was walking, he touched and grabbed things, always resulting with a smash on the floor or on his head. Some of Freddie's accidents were funny, like when something soft fell on him and he made a funny face, but there were others when a lamp fell on his head and he needed a stitch or two.

Tanya stepped to the counter of her department and relieved a part-timer named Tom. She picked up the sale markdown that he started for her. The rest of the day was easy until after 3 P.M. when customers came in for the sale, but Tanya didn't mind. It gave her a break from thinking about Danny.

* * *

About a year ago, Tanya woke up in the middle of the night to hear Danny screaming. She entered the living room and found him on the floor, wide-awake and bleeding from the arm. Tanya wanted to bring him to the hospital but he insisted on staying home. She helped him into the bathroom and nursed the wound. It looked like a large animal bite; like a wolf or dog left four canine teeth punctures in his forearm.

Tanya asked Danny what happened. Danny told her that he heard something out in the living room and investigated, thinking it was one of the Beings. But it wasn't. It was something else altogether. In fact, Danny didn't even get a good look at what attacked him. He said it moved fast like a vicious animal.

A few weeks later Danny started to get paranoid. Instead of sleepwalking, playing, he moved with a purpose. He was frightened of something. Danny started securing the house, protecting them from something that only he saw or felt was out there trying to get him. Whenever Tanya asked him about it, he turned quiet and secretive.

Tanya later found out that it was nothing new. Danny's brother, Ray, was doing the same thing. Ray was bitten by something that same year. He adjusted his house and protected himself from the same monsters that haunted Danny.

Tanya asked Ray what was going on with them, but he wasn't sure. Ray had a theory that it was something hereditary. Bernard, Ray and Danny's father, experienced the same symptoms as them before he killed himself.

Tanya felt helpless and scared. This was out of her league, and she had no one to confide in. Her mother, after finding a new husband for the third time, moved ten years ago to Orange County in California, and Danny's mother died five years ago, finally finding relief from the depression she lived with after her husband's suicide. Tanya feared that she was going to follow the same path as Danny's mother.

* * *

Tanya left work at 8 P.M. and drove straight home. She parked the car on the cracked driveway and headed up to the door. Tanya tried to walk in, but the door was planked up. She figured Danny would have fixed it by now.

Tanya went to the back door and entered the house. She expected Danny home with Freddie, watching television with him on the floor, but no one was around. Worried, she went to the phone and called Ray's house. He picked up on the first ring.

"Ray, it's me. Is Freddie there?"

"Sure is. What happened?"

"Danny didn't come by to pick him up?"

"Nope."

"Well, where is he?"

"I figured that there was traffic on the Turnpike," Ray offered.

Tanya said that she would be right there.

On the way, Tanya came up with a few possible scenarios of where Danny could be. All of which were bad. Danny could have fallen asleep at the wheel and drove into a car accident, or some drunk could have knocked him off the road. Maybe there was an accident at work. His arm could have been caught in the crusher at the back of the truck. It happened to one of his co-workers a few months ago (took his arm off at the elbow and almost bled to death.)

When Tanya arrived, Ray was waiting for her on the front lawn, smoking a cigarette. Ray smiled and waved as he walked to her car.

"That was fast."

"Ray, I'm so sorry."

"It's okay. I like spending time with him," Ray said. "Besides, tomorrow is my day off." Ray worked the morning shift at the local Pathmark where he chopped up meat for the deli department. He kidded around with people and told them that he understood what it was like to be a serial killer, hacking and chopping at dead flesh. People walked away and gave Ray a weird look. He just smiled and waved, getting off on their reaction.

From the house, Freddie came out with his school backpack on and a bunch of papers in his hand. "Hey, Mom," he screamed at her.

Tanya kneeled down and opened her arms for a hug.

"How was your day, sweetie?" Tanya asked.

"Alright."

"Do all your homework."

"Yeah, Uncle Ray helped me."

"Ah, not by much," Ray said, rubbing Freddie's brown-haired head.

"Look what we did." Freddie showed her the papers under the streetlight's glow. They were cartoon style drawings of Ray's white cat, Michelina. "This one here really happened. Michelina was reaching for a fuzzy toy mouse on the top of the fireplace and knocked over a glass. She really did make that face."

"That Michelina," Tanya said. "She's a silly cat, huh?"

"Can we get a cat, mom?"

"Oh, honey. You know your father is allergic."

"Maybe he can get a shot, or something."

"We'll talk about it."

Freddie turned to Ray in disappointment and said, "That's another way of saying 'no'."

"You know you can see Michelina whenever you want," Ray offered. "She always asks about you."

"Okay," Freddie said, slumming.

Tanya thanked Ray again and took Freddie home. When Freddie asked her where his father was, Tanya told him that he got stuck in traffic. He should be home soon.

* * *

By the time Danny came home, Freddie was asleep in bed, and Tanya was in the living room with the television keeping her company. It was eleven at night. With the wettest pair of eyes, Tanya looked at Danny.

"I'm sorry," he said, entering through the back door and not able to look at her.

"Where were you?"

Danny searched for words, trying to come up with something. "I can't lie to you."

"That's good. Then tell me."

"I was out."

"Where."

"I'm. . .trying to get help for us."

"That's great," Tanya said, sarcastically. "But don't you think you can tell me where you were?"

"No. Not yet. I'm sorry."

Danny walked to the bedroom.

Tanya, feeling tired and angry, curled up on the couch and went to sleep.

* * *

Tanya and Danny slept in separate rooms for the rest of the week. While she slept on the couch Tanya woke and saw Danny in a state of paranoia and fear, roaming the room. Sometimes he camped out on a kitchen chair in front of the door and waited with a knife in his hand. Other times, he searched the house, looking for a threat.

That weekend Danny removed the planks from the front door. Freddie stood by his side and helped, gathering and holding the tools that his father needed. Tanya watched them from the kitchen and saw how gentle Danny acted with his son. For a moment she felt a pang of jealousy. It looked like they were sharing something only they could understand.

It ate her up not knowing where Danny was till eleven at night. Tanya knew he wasn't with another woman or hanging out with his friends. She believed him when he told her that he was trying to get help, but from who?

Tanya finally found a clue when she gathered a wash down in the basement. Tanya searched Danny's shirt pockets and found a business card:

DR. TARALLAB
SOMNAMBULIST

* * *

The address on the business card was in town. She turned off Route 9 to a small block of stores and parked her car in the lot. There were four stores, but only two of them were occupied. One was a record store, The White Noise Maker, with a big cassette on the roof and the other, with an empty store in between, was a photocopy center.

Tanya walked to the empty store at the end. The business card said the doctor's office was at 346 Route 9 South. The number at the top of the glass door said the same. It was abandoned. Brown paper bags and smeared soap covered the windows. A "For Rent" sign was attached to the locked door.

She entered the White Noise Maker. Husker Due came out of the speakers. Shelved cassettes and posters covered the walls. The room was only ten feet wide and two yards long, just barely giving people room to move down the aisle and look through the wooden browsers of records in the center. Immediately to the right, she saw a heavy man with a dark brown beard writing something down on a ledger and sifting through some tapes.

"Hi, can I ask you a question?" Tanya asked.

"You can ask me whatever you want," Danny Westerberg said from behind the counter, dropping his tapes and offering his hand in greeting.

Tanya smiled, flattered by the attention and not used to getting any in a while. "I'm afraid it has nothing to do with music," she warned.

"Then, yes. I am free for dinner"

"Um, I'm afraid that's not it, either."

Danny made a fake frown and sat back on his stool. "Okay. Shoot."

"That store on the end, the one that's empty, have you ever seen a doctor's office there?"

"Nope. I've been here for a year and a half. There has never been a doctor's office here. But there is one just further down the highway," he offered.

"Thank you."

Tanya left the store and went back to her car. Her watch said it was just after six. If Danny was coming here after work, then he should be here soon, she thought. Tanya took the business card out of her pocket and studied it. Maybe it was a decoy to steer Tanya away from where Danny really was. This office space was hardly the kind of place a legitimate doctor would hold a session. Plus, it was for rent.

She saw his car pull up. Danny parked in front of the building, left the car, and entered the office.

Entered the office?

Tanya swore that it was locked.

She left the car and walked to the building. Tanya stopped at the door and found it ajar. Tanya stepped inside, letting the parking lot lights shine in. It was as she expected: dark, dusty, and abandoned.

"Danny," she called out.

No one answered.

Tanya took a brick from the floor and propped it in front of the door, holding it wide open. She walked deeper into the room and looked around. Tanya called Danny's name a few more times, but there was still no answer.

At the back of the room was an entrance. The light from the front door didn't reach that far and all she saw was pitch black. But Tanya heard something. A wheezing.

"Danny?"

The wheezing grew stronger and closer.

Tanya ran out of the abandoned office. She didn't stop until she was inside her car. Tanya looked up at the office and saw a distorted, hulking figure hidden in shadow close the door.

* * *

Tanya and Ray waited all night for Danny to come home. She told her brother-in-law what happened at the abandoned office. He listened and asked questions about this Doctor Tarallab. Tanya had no answers, but she told him how she felt. When Tanya drove home, her body broke out into chills. The wheezing sound from deep in the abandoned office invaded her head, making it ache, reaching all the way to her stomach. Tanya stopped the car and puke on the side of Route 9 while traffic passed her by without a care in the world.

"I felt such an evil in there," Tanya finished.

"And you didn't see anyone?" Ray asked.

"I'm not sure. I felt like there was someone in there with me."

Ray paced around the room and receded into himself. Tanya watched him, nervously shaking her crossed legs. "What?" Tanya asked him.

"It's a pattern."

"What do you mean?"

"Our father did the same. I don't know if he was seeing a doctor. He never believed in them. But he was acting weird before he killed himself. He disappeared every once and a while. Mom tried to hide it on us, but... Shit, you can't hide stuff like that."

"If it is a pattern, then..." Tanya covered her mouth as a horrid thought ran through her head.

"No." Ray took her hand. "We don't know for sure. Okay?"

Tanya rubbed tears from her eyes and nodded her head. "Yeah. We don't know for sure," she said.

* * *

Danny came home that night at 3:32 A.M. and found Ray and Tanya. They sat on the couch and looked at him. Danny cracked a smile and said, "I guess the first thing I should think is that my wife and brother are having an affair."

No one laughed.

Danny's smile dropped. He locked the door.

Ray stepped up to him, keeping a distance.

"We could think the same of you," Ray said.

Danny exhaled and shook his head. "Man, I'm not fucking around." Danny stepped around his brother and walked to Tanya. "What, is that what you think is going on with me?"

Tanya, tired and scared, adverted her eyes away from Danny. "No," she said. "I know exactly where you been."

Danny looked away.

"You want to tell us about this Doctor Tarallab?" Ray asked.

"What's there to tell?" Danny asked.

"Jesus," Ray spat.

Tanya stepped up to Danny and grabbed his hand. "Please, Danny. Look at me. Look in my eyes and tell me what you see."

"I see the woman that I love," Danny said.

"What else? Can you see how scared I am?"

"I do. But, I also see a woman who I know will do anything for me, who will love me till the day I die. A woman who wants to help me, but she could never completely understand what is going on in my head, because it is impossible even for me to understand what is going on."

"Is this Tarallab understanding? Does he know what is going on in your head?"

"Yes."

"Then why didn't you tell me about him?"

"I'm not supposed to tell you about him. He didn't want me too."

"What the fuck is that supposed to mean," Ray jumped in. "We're your fuckin' family. I'm your brother. We see the same things in our sleep..."

"It is an isolated process. You don't achieve revelation in a group. This is not a religion," Danny pleaded. "I have to go through it alone."

"Did he tell you that?" Tanya asked.

Danny walked away from her, heading for the bedroom. "I'm tired. I have to go to work in a few hours."

When the bedroom door closed, Ray threw his arms in the air. Tanya watched the hall. Her eyes were wet and dazed. Ray took his jacket and keys from the closet.

"I don't know what to do," Ray offered.

"That's not him?"

Ray kissed Tanya's cheek and stepped into her view, trying to get her attention. "Listen, we'll try again later. All right? I'm gonna check out this Doctor Tarallab. While I do that just watch him. Okay?"

Tanya remained still.

Ray left.

"That's not him," Tanya said.

* * *

As the week went on, Danny stayed away all night and then came home the next morning. He was too tired to go to work and called in sick. Tanya wanted to argue with him, but she didn't. She knew it would get her nowhere. Danny hardly acknowledged her. His morning smiles disappeared as well as the way he looked at her: as if she was the hottest thing he had ever seen. In a way, Tanya felt like she was in mourning. All that was left of Danny was a shell. And, just when she was getting an idea about kicking him out of the house for a while, Danny disappeared for a few nights. His job called for him, wondering where he was. Tanya stalled them as long as she could, telling his boss that Danny was very sick and unable to get out of bed. Tanya told Danny's boss that she was thinking about taking Danny to the hospital if things didn't get better. It seemed to satisfy the suspicion.

When it came to Freddy, all was normal. Danny responded to him. Whenever Danny was home, he spent time with his son. They played and drew, having the best time.

Tanya, whenever she witnessed them, laughed to herself. No matter how bad things turned for Danny and herself, the boys club stuck together.

Why?

At the end of the week, Ray came to the house while Danny was missing. Ray found nothing about a Doctor Tarallab. When he checked into the address where the sessions were held, the location was still for rent. The owner of the building told Ray that it had been empty for six months now, but he had a potential client lined up.

A doctor?

Nope. A pottery store.

Ray checked with an old girlfriend who was a nurse at Freehold Hospital and she never heard of a Doctor Tarallab. The nurse even asked the other doctors. Ray asked her if she checked the psyche ward. Yep, there, too. Nothing.

It all came down to nothing.

* * *

Then, she found it.

It looked old and used. There were scratches on the handle where, Tanya assumed, the serial number was supposed to be. Tanya was ignorant about guns, but she guessed it was a police issued .38 caliber.

She found it in the closet. It was not in a box or wrapped in a dirty rag. It sat on the top shelf, out in the open.

Tanya took it down and held it with three fingers pinched around the bottom of the handle. It was loaded with bullets. Tanya wanted to take it and bury it in the backyard.

But she placed it back.

Tanya was too scared to break the world, the pattern. She was frightened of what Danny might do if it was fractured by the slightest change.

Tanya closed the bedroom door, sat down on the bed, and cried.

* * *

A few days later, they awakened from the nightmare.

Tanya slept in bed one Saturday morning when she found Danny with her. He was down between her legs, tasting and savoring her. Tanya couldn't say a word. She didn't want to say a word. When Danny brought her to orgasm and moved up to meet her mouth with his, Tanya saw the smile on his face.

"I love you, Tanya," Danny whispered.

She smiled at him.

They connected the rest of the morning.

* * *

Danny made Tanya and Freddie breakfast and apologized to them for the way he acted the last few months. He promised that, as of today, things were going to be different. Danny wasn't cured yet, but his therapy was coming to a close. Doctor Tarallab told Danny that he didn't need his services anymore after he completed Final Phase.

"So what do you have to do?" she asked, testing and humoring him. "Is it like a twelve step program?"

"No, not really," Danny said with a mouthful of pancakes. "More like one step."

Tanya wasn't sure that she believed him, but she was glad that he was going to stop his old ways and return to a normal life.

Danny turned to Freddie. "Hey! How would you like to go to Great A. today?"

"Yeah!" screamed Freddie.

Danny turned to Tanya for her approval. She smiled and said,

"Okay."

They rode all the rides together. At least, the rides that Freddie was tall enough to get on. They had a good time as a family. There was no boys club, and Tanya felt convinced that things really were different.

That night Danny took them out to Friendly's and then a movie. Freddie picked the movie. It was a little silly and definitely made for a child. They had a good time.

When they put Freddie to bed, Tanya and Danny curled up on the couch and watched television. He promised in her ear that things were going to be different and perfect in the morning. In the middle of "Saturday Night Live," Tanya fell asleep in Danny's arms.

* * *

She woke up a few hours later. Tanya was still on the couch, but Danny was gone. There was a gunshot from down the hall. Things fell apart, again.

II

Fire in the Rain
(1996)

Daryl Hersh sat in a chair with his legs under the desk in his one room apartment. His right hand held a pencil, trying to write fast enough to catch up with his brain. The sun had just set, darkening the room, but it didn't slow his pace. Early Lemonheads blared out of the stereo speakers from across the room, enhancing his concentration.

When Daryl reached the end of the chapter, he looked over at the digital clock next to his bed and saw it was 6:30 P.M.

He was late.

Daryl promised to meet Liz at 6:00 P.M at her apartment. He jumped out of the chair and released an aggravated breath; not because of the rush he was about to start, but for the reason Liz was going to assume he was late for.

He changed out of his work clothes (black jeans and black polo shirt with the Shiny Disc logo on the breast) and dropped them on the floor. Daryl then picked the shirt up and gave it a quick smell. He placed it on the bed, deciding it had a few more days of wear before customers looked at him funny. Daryl slipped on a pair of blue jeans, a Pixies T, and some fresh deodorant. At the door, he swiped on his denim jacket and black cap and left.

From 33rd Street and 3rd Ave., Daryl walked to 4th Ave. and 21st Street. He moved fast and weaved through New Yorkers, avoiding eye contact.

At Liz's building, he pressed the buzzer. Jeanie's voice came out of the static-filled speaker.

"Is that you?" she asked in annoyance.

Daryl never liked her much either.

"Yeah."

"You mean, yes."

"Don't give me any shit, Jeanie."

"She's not here. She left without you," Jeanie said nonchalantly.

Daryl moved his mouth closer to the speaker.

"That's bullshit," Daryl told her.

The door buzzed, and Daryl entered. He went up the stairs to the third floor. Liz stood with her arms crossed and her trademark sneer on her face by her open apartment door.

"The movie starts at 7:15, Daryl."

"Yes. I know. I'm sorry."

"Did you get held up at work?"

"No." Daryl kissed her cheek. The anger on her face remained. "What? I'm sorry," he pleaded. "Jesus. It was not like I was with another woman or something."

"No, you were with some stupid cat. P.S.: don't get Jesus involved in this."

"Listen," Daryl said. "It's not stupid. How would you like it if I made fun of the scripts you wrote? Your art?"

"That's the thing, Daryl. I do art. That little thing you do is... Jesus, it's meaningless. You're 22, it's time to get focused," she said.

"I thought we weren't going to bring Jesus into this." Daryl, depression setting in, looked away. "Are we going out or what?" he asked.

"Yeah, I guess."

She closed the door, and they left. When Liz and Daryl stepped on the street and started walking to the theater, Daryl said, "You seem a little bit more pissed at me than usual."

"I just hate to see you waste your time writing that crap," she said.

"Yeah, well."

"You're a talented guy, Daryl. You should focus your talents on the stuff you do for Stove Topp," she offered.

"I just do that for exposure and what little perks Tony can give me." Daryl shrugged. "Besides, I have other things to express besides the black shit that is inside of me."

"Black shit sells. If I didn't write black shit, I wouldn't have sold my script to that asshole."

"Oh, shit," Daryl just remembered. "How did the meeting go?"

"Terrible. It felt like a gynecology exam by Freddy Krueger. He gave me these notes on what he wants in the re-writes," Liz said. "It's fuckin' outrageous. He's turning it into a new movie. What the fuck did he buy it for anyway?"

"Did you tell him?"

"No, I want this. It's my first sale. Do you know how many people in our graduating class are still whoring themselves just to get a query letter read? This is a big chance. I'm not going to fuck it up. But I can still be pissed about it."

They were eight minutes late for the movie, but they were still on time for the feature. Daryl and Liz took their seats at the end of the previews.

"See, we're okay," Daryl offered.

She nodded, distracted.

Daryl placed his arm around her. Liz relaxed and ate from the bag of popcorn on his lap. By the end of the movie, their hands secretly connected in the dark, and they smiled at each other for no apparent reason.

* * *

Daryl took her to McGowan's Pub to eat and listen to Irish folk music. Daryl gave her plenty of attention. He held her hand across the table and snuck her a kiss whenever he could. Daryl was not at all embarrassed by public affection, especially when he felt like he was falling in love.

As bossy and moody as Liz Vasquez was she also had her good points. Liz supported his other pursuits. Stove Topp was a zine based out of Manhattan. Daryl wrote short horror stories and drew illustrations to go with them. It didn't pay, but it was just popular enough that people recognized Daryl from his work.

Daryl met Liz at the School of Visual Arts. Daryl majored in Fine Arts while Liz studied Film. One day in the crowded lounge, between classes, Daryl sat with his headset on and his sketchpad open in the back booth. Liz took the seat across from him. She held an armful of ¾ inch videotapes and placed them on the table. At first, Daryl didn't notice her, too deep into a sketch, but Liz had a way of getting people's attention. Daryl quickly put the sketchbook away and gave her the attention she wanted. Liz promised to only bother him for 20 minutes while she waited for an available editing room. There was no one in the lounge she wanted to speak to, so would he mind? Not at all, Daryl said.

Liz talked about the short film she was editing and the feature script she was trying to start. Daryl wasn't really paying attention, but listening enough that he could answer her questions. Instead, he focused on her face. Daryl was instantly attracted to her subtle mix of Mexican and Caucasian features.

When Liz was about to leave, Daryl asked if she wanted to hang out some time. She said that would be cool. They went to movies, clubs, friend's parties, and hung out at each other's apartments. Things moved hot and fast; they were pretty much inseparable. They became a couple and they liked it.

But their sex life was a little odd.

Well, their post-sex life. No matter how late it was Daryl would leave or drop her home after they were together. They never really slept overnight together.

Now, a couple of years later, Daryl decided that it was time to let Liz in. When they left McGowan's Pub and started to head to her apartment, Daryl stopped her.

"Let's go back to my place," Daryl said.

"It's late. I don't want to walk back that late," Liz said.

"You don't have to," he said.

She looked at him and smiled.

"Yeah?"

"Yeah," he said.

Daryl smiled back.

* * *

The Beings floated above Daryl while he slept. Their faces were waxy white and smoothed down to reveal the most delicate features. He could never properly describe them or draw them in detail. He always knew them to be kind, and sensed their smiles. Daryl felt no fear whenever the Beings woke him up at night. They never tried to harm him. Although, when he was a child they tried tickling him. Daryl squirmed away and grabbed their soft arms. He felt a warm rush from their bodies, making his muscles relax. It was a dirty trick. Daryl released them and they went right for his ribs, making him fold over and howl in joy.

The Beings were more playful that night while Liz slept unaware next to him. They taunted Daryl, reaching out to tease him and make him get out of the bed. It was stupid and childish, but he didn't care. Daryl followed them out into the other room. One Being hid behind the couch. Daryl snuck up on it. When he reached the couch, Daryl kneeled down and prepared to pounce.

When ready, he sprung over the couch and landed on the hard floor. The Being wasn't there; reality was.

* * *

"Daryl?"

He woke up in his living room. It was still nighttime. Daryl was naked behind the couch. He looked up and saw Liz standing by the bedroom door, hugging and hiding behind it.

"What are you doing?" she asked.

Daryl stood up in embarrassment. He had no idea what he was doing. Daryl felt cloudy and tired.

"What did it look like I was doing?" he treaded carefully.

"It looked like you were playing hide and seek."

"Well, there you go," he said. Daryl, with as much dignity he could muster being naked, walked back to the bedroom. "Back to bed, huh?" he suggested.

Daryl walked past Liz at the threshold and saw her move away from him. He stopped and turned to her. "Aren't you tired?"

"Do you do this every night?" Liz asked.

Daryl looked away, embarrassed.

"Yeah, I guess so."

Liz stood there and looked at the floor, thinking. Liz then smiled at him and walked to the bed, keeping a safe distance from Daryl.

Daryl kissed Liz goodnight.

"Are you alright?" Daryl asked.

"Yeah. I'm fine," she assured him.

They slept with a distance between them.

* * *

Liz was quiet the next morning. Daryl quickly noticed it and tried to keep last night out of any conversation. Daryl, like every morning after a sleepwalking episode, remembered what he did the previous night.

"So, what do you want to do for breakfast?" Daryl asked.

"I have to get started on those re-writes," Liz said, half-dressed by the bed. "That bastard wants them by the end of the week."

Daryl, on the bed, looked dejected.

Liz stepped up to Daryl and wrapped her arms around him.

"Make me something tonight?" Liz asked.

"Okay."

Liz left without a kiss goodbye.

Daryl dressed for work then made a bagel with cream cheese for breakfast. He munched on it at the kitchen table, and listened to the neighbors play Cajun music.

He then prepared his submission for St. Peter's Press. Daryl had a good feeling for this publisher. They were big on printing slightly obscure stuff, especially children's books. He shopped his book to publishers for the last year and before that, he shopped it to agents. Mostly, no one gave any interest to his queries. He did have one or two bites to read the whole book, but when they sent it back, they told Daryl that it wasn't something for them to pursue at the time.

Maybe Liz was right. Maybe the publishers were looking for black shit or overly happy characters that they could print to the world. Who wants to read a kids book about a cat and her life in a suburban house?

Stamped and sealed, Daryl packed the envelope and lunch into his backpack. He left the apartment and dropped his future career into the mailbox.

* * *

Kate Bacon was 23 years old and went to the same art school as Daryl. She was a phenomenal artist. Kate looked at an object once and copied it to the finest detail on the canvas. Instructors teased Kate and, with contempt, called her a copy machine. It pissed Kate off to have people that she looked up to be so mad at her. Kate once told Daryl it was stupid for them to feel that way. She wasn't impressed with her duplication skills, figuring the skill was something that she didn't need to develop. Kate wanted to do more. When she graduated, Kate started to draw and paint like a child, staying far away from detailed reality.

Using her new child-like technique, Kate sold a few paintings and had a few shows. Did the money come rolling in? No. Kate sold enough that she only had to work part-time. That was time too much. Kate hated working. The idea of serving the public enraged her. There was only one other path for her. Kate turned to the world's oldest profession, but not in the Catholic sense.

Kate reported six nights a week to a brownstone apartment building where she worked for Mrs. Bucket. She was a Madam, but she didn't sell sex, she sold pain. Men came in and paid Kate (as well as other women who worked there) to humiliate them and make them feel physical pain. It was perfect. Kate never had to touch them in any way except with an instrument. She made enough money to pay her bills.

Kate painted and rented videos during the day. She was big on camp and bad taste. Kate treasured every film with the Troma name on it and bootlegs of John Water's films.

That day, Kate stumbled on a sidewalk sale on 6th Ave. She made a grand discovery. "Meet the Feebles" was nestled in between a bunch of porno tapes. She quickly snatched the bootleg up. Kate made the hairy guy missing one leg test it on his television/VCR set up and found the tape to be pristine and widescreen.

Kate paid the man ten dollars and ran to the Shiny Disc.

"Darry, Darry, Darry."

"Katy, Katy, Katy."

Kate shoved the tape in Daryl's face as he blistered up compact discs at the back of the store. A recently dropped shipment surrounded Daryl. He looked bored as hell.

"Meet the who?" he asked.

"Feebles. You're coming over tonight to watch this with me," Kate declared.

"Can't. I promised Liz that I'd do something with her tonight," he explained. "Something special."

"Oh, fuck her. This is important."

"So is this."

"What?"

Daryl looked away, pissing Kate off.

"It's not friggin' important, is it?"

"I'm making her something for dinner," he confessed. "It's important for our relationship."

"You fucked up, huh?"

"I don't want to talk about it." Daryl picked up a pile of blistered CDs and walked down the aisle.

Kate followed.

"Daryl, I'm sure you didn't do anything wrong," she said. "You're, like, an over grown Boy Scout."

"Uh, huh."

"She's putting a power trip on you and you let her do it. Plus, you have low self-esteem."

"What person in our generation doesn't," Daryl countered.

Kate stepped in front of his face.

"Cutie, you're a good person. You could do better."

Daryl took a breath and smiled.

"I'll call you tonight. Okay?"

"Okay." Kate kissed his cheek and left the store. Customers watched her sing "My Way," opera style, on the way out.

Daryl smiled.

* * *

Liz left a message on Daryl's answering machine. She asked him over her place instead. Don't dress up, Liz stressed.

Weird.

He arrived at the apartment to find Jeanie at the door. She looked at him as if Daryl had an arm growing out of his head. Daryl gave her a big awkward smile.

"Hi, Jeanie," he smiled. "How are ya?"

"Hi," she said.

"Aren't you going to let me in?"

Jeanie stepped out of his way. Daryl saw her wander away, absently twirling her dreaded hair. She looked nervous, or scared, about something. She made Daryl nervous.

"Have a seat," Jeanie said. She left the room and entered Liz's bedroom. Daryl sat on the couch and looked around the apartment. It looked the same as always, small and cluttered. He noticed his legs jumping up and down. Daryl stopped them when Liz cautiously entered the room. Liz tried to smile for Daryl, but her fear showed more.

Liz was dressed for bed or a night at home. She sat next to Daryl on the couch, keeping a foot of space between them. It took Liz a while to say what she had to say but, as Daryl knew of her, she got it out.

It was bad.

* * *

Kate sat on the couch while Daryl lay across it with his head on her lap. 50-hour candles that had been burning for 20 hours lit the room. There was a mix of fruity and perfume smells in the air. The Cramps came out of the stereo speakers. They were just loud enough to cover any silence in the conversation.

"I should have expected it, you know," Daryl said.

"She's a bitch. This is a good thing for you," Kate said. "If she isn't able to deal with that part of your life, then she was not meant to be in it."

"Scared of me. She was scared to go back to bed with me, but she was also scared to leave. Like I was going to hurt her or something."

"She doesn't really know you," she explained.

"Jeanie told her that she knew a guy back home who was a sleepwalker and he murdered his parents in his sleep one night," Daryl said. "The guy didn't even remember that he did it. He's in jail now."

"Do you think it was true?"

"I don't know."

"Yeah, but you always remember the next morning," Kate reminded. "It's apples and oranges. Besides, she is a freak, her and that dick-of-a-roommate. You're not dangerous, Daryl."

"Am I? Well, from this day on I'm swearing off women. They're too much heartache."

"Don't be a dick, Daryl."

"I just wish my life wasn't so...fucked."

* * *

Eleven years ago, a ten-year-old boy was found in a cargo train in Ontario, Canada. He slept in an empty car that came from South Carolina, U.S.A. Jerzy Page, who worked security that night, found him nestled in the corner of the car. Jerzy shined the light on the boy and woke him up. He was dressed like he had been on the street for years. His hair was blonde and cropped. The boy didn't look scared, just confused. He asked the boy, in French and English, his name, and where he was from, but the boy just looked at Jerzy. In English, the boy said he did not know.

The police came and took the boy away. A social worker named Denise Mascis came by and, with the police, tried to figure out where the boy came from. They ran his prints in the computers and flashed his picture around all the towns near and where the train stopped.

Nothing.

The boy lived at Mr. and Mrs. Jimenez's house during the search. They were old at the game of foster care and often opened their home to lost children until they found a more permanent place to live.

Denise found the boy in the living room. He watched a video called "D.A.R.Y.L." that the Jimenez' rented for the kids. Denise sat down on the floor next to him and waited for the movie to end before she broke the news.

The boy looked a little upset when she told him that the search for his family was over.

"It's not like I can remember what I'm missing," he offered.

Denise smiled.

"I've arranged for you to live someplace else."

"The Jimenez's don't want me to stay?" he asked.

"They only offer their home for short-term visits," Denise explained. "Full-time is too exhausting for their age. They used to, though. But those kids are all grown up now."

The boy looked away. "That's too bad. I guess I missed the deadline, huh."

"But there is an institute that is ready to accept you. You can live there with other children, and they will put you in school. Plus, the best part is, they'll help you find new parents."

"I guess that would be good."

"What's wrong, sweetie?" Denise asked.

"If I can remember who my parents are, can I go back and live with them?"

"Sure you can. That is, if they can take care of you."

"What do you mean?"

"Well, we don't know why you were placed on that train," Denise said. "They could of done it to you, or something could have happened to them, or you might have been kidnapped and the bad man might have put you there."

Denise knew none of those possibilities was true. Someone,

anyone, could have responded to the search tactics. Denise felt the boy was not supposed to be returned.

"Why can't I remember?" he said in frustrated tears.

"You will," she comforted. "The doctor said it will come back to you one day. Amnesia isn't permanent."

Denise placed her arm around the boy and sat there for a few minutes until he stopped crying.

"Now." Denise opened her brief case and took out some documents. "We need to tell the world who you are."

"I need a name," he stated to her.

She smiled at his confidence. "What would you like it to be?"

"Daryl," he offered.

"Like the movie?"

"Yeah."

"But, you're not a robot."

"I know that. I like the name."

Denise wrote it down.

"And your last name?" she asked.

"Hersh. I saw it on T.V. the other night. I like it. Daryl Hersh."

"Congratulations, you have an identity."

* * *

Daryl woke up on Kate's couch. He was in the same position, but Kate was on the floor. She kneeled down next to him with his palm opened in her own hand.

"Hm, what?" Daryl looked at her with tired eyes.

Kate dropped his hand.

"Jesus. Scare me, why don't you?" she said. "I thought you were sleeping."

"I was." Daryl sat up. "I'm up now."

"You can crash here if you want," Kate offered.

"No thanks."

Daryl reached for his boots and slipped them on.

Kate, with her arms propping her up from behind, sat back on the floor. "You know you have some interesting lines there."

Daryl tied his boots and flinched at her.

"What do you mean?"

Kate took Daryl's hand and opened the palm. "Your life line is odd. For one thing, your marriage line intercepts your life line pretty early."

"How is that odd?"

"Dippy, you just swore off women tonight."

"Oh, right."

"The other thing is that your life line breaks off. It goes long in one line and short on the other. That makes no sense. The lines in your hand are supposed to map out your fate. See here, you're suppose to have three kids."

"Jesus, three?" he exclaimed.

"The second life line says you're going to die. The life lines aren't suppose to fork like that," Kate explained.

Daryl took his hand back and moved for his denim jacket.

"It's probably just some birth defect," he said.

"Yeah, maybe."

Kate studied her own palm.

"My life line is very short," she said "So I'm gonna die soon. Maybe in a couple of years. It's hard to say."

Daryl turned to her.

"That's not funny."

"If I'm meant to die, I'm gonna die, Daryl," Kate said. "You can't stop fate."

"If you die, I'll come after you and kill you," Daryl promised.

Kate looked at him and smiled sweetly.

"You all right?" Daryl asked. "Want me to stay a little longer?"

"No, go home. It's okay. I'm gonna do some painting. It always pushes the demons away for a while," Kate said, getting on her feet. "You'll just break my concentration."

Daryl kissed the top of her head. "See ya."

"Night, cutie."

Daryl left.

* * *

Tony Buitoni was one slick motherfucker.

He was born and raised in New York. Tony witnessed and profited from all the major New York scenes for the last twenty years. When punk and art hit the streets in the seventies, he embraced it with the zine Stove Topp. It documented all the artists and featured prominent and impressive works of fiction. The zine was respected and recognized as a powerful marketing tool for artist. When no-wave came out in the early eighties, Stove Topp covered it when no one else would, making it ballsier than The Voice.

Was money being made?

Just by Tony and it was enough for him to get by. He was never after fame; he just wanted to do something he loved and he loved his job. Tony received free promos from local publishers and musicians. He usually used these promotional items to pay for the fiction that ran in his issues. The contributors didn't complain.

Daryl Hersh stepped into his office to drop off his latest work for the next issue.

"Tony, we've been working together for over 2 years now." Daryl sat in the beanbag chair across from the older man's desk.

"Great fuckin' years, Daryl. I don't like to reveal this to my contributors, but my circulation did go up when your work got going."

"I don't want to take complete control or credit for that."

"Daryl, when I printed your first story the reader response was beyond belief. Un-fuckin'-believable. You are a keeper, my man. I'm just glad I snagged ya and that you're willing."

"Well, I like what I do," Daryl said. He squirmed.

"Like, huh?" Tony asked. "But you don't love."

"Not lately. I mean... I don't know. I would like to change my content."

Tony looked at him suspiciously. "To what?"

"I like the horror that I write..."

"So do thousands of readers. It fits the format of the issues. There is a lot of dark shit out there, Daryl. The music scene is certainly filled with it." Tony tossed a CD at Daryl. "You know them?"

Daryl looked at the case: Paw Padds. He smiled at the coincidence. The cover had a distorted and blurred photo of a close-up of something fleshy and pink.

"What is that?" Daryl asked.

"Yeah, I was freaked out, too. I thought it was a fat pussy or something. Sadly, it is not. It's what the words on the corner says it is."

"It says Paw Padds."

"That's what it is," Tony said. "See the nails."

"Oh."

"It's a chick band. Hot bunch. And I don't mean the music." Tony watched Daryl open the case. "Don't bother looking for photos, there are none. Photo shy. But I met them. I did an interview for the next issue. Lead singer is hot. Got the best heart-shaped ass you will ever see. Her name's Belinda Kastner."

"She showed her ass to you in an interview?" Daryl asked.

"Shit. I wish."

"So, what's your point?"

Tony leaned forward, serious.

"My point is: These chicks are dark. Not just lyrically but musically. They do things with their instruments in such a low-fi way that they could put Richards and Townsend to shame. With a little money they could be the next Dinosaur, Jr. or Sonic Youth. This is great shit. It's dark shit because it challenges. Just like you, Daryl. Your fiction challenges and you have a voice. I understand you want to express yourself in other ways, but I can't let you do it here."

Daryl reached into his bag and took out his manuscript.

"Would you read it, please? Just read it, I think you'll change your mind."

Tony took it. "Okay."

Daryl handed back the CD.

"Keep it," Tony said. "Perks and payment, man."

* * *

Daryl wondered about his book. He mailed it to St. Peter's Press five months ago and expected some kind of confirmation. He called them up and made contact with the editor's secretary. She told Daryl that they received the submission. That was all. Did they read it? Did they put it on the pile of other manuscripts that they requested from would-be authors? Maybe it was in the garbage.

He hung up the phone. Daryl felt no better. When he sat on the couch and turned on the television, Daryl concluded that he was going to work at the Disc for the rest of his life.

He was an assistant manager for over a year. Daryl followed the usual pattern of a manager. He started the job to support himself through school and to cover the expenses that his loans and scholarships did not handle. He was a clerk that worked the register. Daryl handled every kind of crisis and became trusted by the management staff. Right after graduation, his manager, Johnny Johnson, offered him an assistant manager position that was recently available. Lewis Sampson, the previous assistant manager, was fired and arrested for gradually stealing a few thousand dollars worth of CDs. Daryl felt sorry for Lewis and was a little upset. He knew Lewis had trouble with money. His mother was in and out of the hospital and his father died the year before, leaving the family a huge debt in credit cards and mortgages. Plus, Lewis was in a money hole himself, but with a more unofficial and dirty moneylender.

Daryl took the management position. He received more responsibility, and it took him off the register. He quickly grew bored and lodged himself into a daily pattern. Daryl then decided to learn Johnny's tasks just so he could do something new. Johnny did not mind, he said he could use the help. Over-worked. Under-paid. Johnson appreciated the extra effort, and showed Daryl how to run the store, hoping he will get his own in the future.

Daryl never imagined he would get his own store. He sure as hell did not want it. But maybe he would need it.

A career as a writer did not seem possible at that moment in his life. He did have a little recognition with his printed works in Stove Topp but it did not make submitting stories to mags that were more mainstream any easier or made stronger impressions with the publishers he queried.

His book did not exactly follow his other works. It was a kid's book with illustrations. It was not something you would expect from someone who wrote short horror stories. Liz said that publishers probably thought Daryl was some degenerate who wrote kid's books to lure children to the grave. She also told him, repeatedly, that he was not going to get far selling children's fiction when he had such a strong background in horror. Daryl had a few ideas for horror novels, but the images and stories for kids were too strong to put on hold. He secretly wrote the kid's book throughout his relationship with Liz. She eventually found out about it and put him down. Daryl explained how his heart felt and how he thought that this was the best route for himself. Liz told him that she understood, but you cannot break into the publishing world with your heart, just your brain. You have to be clever and give people what they want.

Daryl disbelieved that. People had no idea what they wanted. They believed what you told them to believe. If one person said that so-and-so's book was great that person was going to read it and say the same thing. They might not agree, but they would be too scared to disagree with mass majority.

Now, sitting in the dark, alone, depressed and discouraged, he started to feel that Liz was right.

* * *

Daryl woke up in the bathroom one Friday morning. He did not remember right away how he got there but, like always, it came to him at breakfast. Daryl thought it was funny how memory always came to him at breakfast. Maybe food was a memory releaser. But if that was true then he would have remembered where he came from a long time ago.

Daryl went to work and opened the store. Johnny usually opened on Fridays but he had tickets for a KISS reunion concert and expected to be out all night. Daryl covered his shift and closed the store the night before.

Johnny Johnson was a major KISS fan. He had all the vinyl printed from different countries, and every kind of collectable that was produced during the seventies. Johnny left work yesterday in full Gene Simmons make-up and leather outfit complete with fake hairy chest and high-heeled devil boots.

"Gonna rock and roll all night long, man," Johnny exclaimed, walking out of the store while confused customers stared at him.

The morning sucked.

The safe was off by fifty dollars. Daryl swore that it was even when he left last night. He checked the deposit and the cash tills. The money was not there. Daryl freaked in the desk chair for a few minutes and then gathered his nerves.

A half hour before the store opened, the phone rang. The opening cashier claimed to be sick. Daryl said fine, but knew it was a bullshit excuse. Smallpox had not been around for a long time, Daryl was sure of that. Daryl then asked if the cashier found anyone to cover for him, he said no. The guy tried. No one picked up their phone.

Figured.

Daryl thought to call and try to get someone in, but figured he would get the same response as the opener. Daryl opened by himself, hoping it would be dead until noon when the second cashier arrived.

Nope.

People came in all morning and asked for the latest Oasis. Daryl explained that it was not coming out until next Tuesday. Like the Shiny Disc wanted, Daryl offered a reservation for the disc. Some customers did. Some declined when they found out they had to place a deposit.

Then a die-hard fan came in.

"No. No. I saw it on MTV this morning that it was already out today," the customer explained with a fake British accent.

The customer took off their mirrored shades and looked at Daryl suspiciously.

"Hey man. Are you, like, hiding it on me? Is this some kind of plan leading to a censorship of an artist?"

Daryl, mouth open in disbelief, looked at the customer.

"I can call the cops, man, and report you," the customer said. "Where is your manager?"

"He's not in until later this afternoon," Daryl said. "I'm all you got."

"This is bullshit, man," he said, heading for the door. "I'm coming back here with the cops."

Daryl wished he did.

Daryl then helped a customer find a Michael Bolton CD that had that popular R&B song that he covered a couple of years ago. While they scanned the disks, Daryl noticed a man with a stuffed shopping bag leaving the store and setting off the alarm. Daryl ran to catch him, but the thief was one with the city street. The Michael Bolton fan thanked Daryl for his help and said he would come by later when he had some money. Daryl wandered over to the rap section to see a big hole where the Gravediggas and Wu-Tang Clan CDs were supposed to be. He realized he was tag-teamed by a couple of thieves.

Things eased a bit when the cashier showed up. Daryl sat in the back to clear his head and catch his breath. Then Johnny came in at 1 o'clock.

"Hey, man, how did it go?" Johnny asked.

"Fucked," Daryl offered.

Johnny shook his head as Daryl went through the morning.

"Were you able to get the store ready for Marcia?" Johnny asked.

"Fuck."

Daryl completely forgot about the District Manager. Marcia was supposed to do an official store visit, which would reflect their raises. Johnny wanted Daryl to double check the planner to make sure the correct advertisements were running and operations were in order. Daryl did none of it.

It was not a good day.

* * *

Daryl wanted to stay home, jerk off, and go to sleep, but Kate had other plans when she called him up on the phone.

"You need to go out, you dumb motherfucker," she kindly explained.

"I don't want to go out. I have plans," Daryl said.

"You can jerk off when you get home."

That was true, Daryl thought.

"I'm not in the mood to deal with people tonight. Please, Kate"

"But Frank Black is playing at B.G.C.B. and this is suppose to be the end of the tour. You are not going to make me miss him."

"You don't need me to go with you."

"If I'm going to pick up a boy-toy, I do," Kate said. "If a cute guy sees me with you, they will definitely see me as looking for someone new."

"Gee, thanks."

"So you'll go?"

"No."

"Please."

"No."

"Pretty please."

"No."

"Pretty please with sugar on top."

"Oh, for fuck's sake. Yes. I'll go."

* * *

B.G.C.B. was packed by the time Kate and Daryl arrived. The room was too small. The stage was right next to the bar. The first thing they did was get drinks while the bartender could still hear them; once the bands started playing it would become a screaming match and the bands always won.

With a half an hour to kill before the opening band, Daryl and Kate sat at a small table in the back by the restrooms. Kate instructed Daryl on how to act with her, as if he was her boyfriend. At first, Daryl was not into it. As Kate moved his arms around like a marionette, he started to loosen up. Daryl acted like a dramatic love fool, laughing in her mouth whenever he tried to kiss her.

It worked.

An androgynistic boy just out of his teens made severe eye contact with Kate as she rested her head on Daryl's shoulder. Kate made secret advances towards the lonely boy in ripped clothes and green hair. As she reached a flirtatious crescendo, Kate excused herself.

Daryl sat alone with his drink. He scanned the room while P.W.E.I. covered the room. Daryl then saw her walk up to him. She was about his age. She had a small cat-like face lightly covered with freckles. Her light brown hair was highlighted red, and she was dressed as if she worked in a factory. Daryl had no idea who she was, but she smiled and waved at him as if they knew each other for years.

"Hi. Mind if I?" she asked, motioning to the chair.

Daryl stood up.

"Um. Sure. It's all yours."

She sat down with her tomato-colored drink, picking her teeth with a straw.

"Am I freaking you out?" she asked.

"Do I know you?" Daryl sat back down.

"I don't know." She showed off an angle of her face. "Do I look familiar?"

Daryl smiled.

"No."

"I know you," she said. "You're Daryl Hersh. Stove Topp."

"Yeah. That's right." He looked away as red filled his cheeks.

"Oh, that's so cute," she screamed. "You're blushing."

Daryl turned redder.

"My God. You're head isn't going to explode, is it?"

Daryl placed his palms on his cheeks.

"No. I hope not.

"I'm sorry. I'll stop. I just wanted to meet you and tell you how cool I think your writings and drawings are," she said. "By the way, my name is Belinda."

Belinda offered her pale, soft hand. They shook.

"You're here with your girlfriend?" she asked.

"No."

"Oh. Then a boyfriend..."

"Oh, no. I'm just here with a friend. She wanted me here to make guys jealous," Daryl explained. "I think it worked."

"So you're not here to see Frank Black or Paw Padds?"

"Nah."

"Don't like the music?"

"Well, I liked the Pixies stuff he did. I haven't heard much of his solo. Paw Padds? Well, to be honest I haven't heard any of their stuff."

Daryl noticed Belinda looking behind him.

"Uh, oh," she said.

"What?"

"There are some girls looking at us."

Daryl turned to them. They were about his age and very different from each other. One girl had teased eighties hair and wore a baby-whore dress. The other was dressed in solid black and wore studded wrists bands and belts. A couple of bright peacock feathers sprouted from her nest-like hair. The two girls at the bar giggled at Daryl and Belinda.

"You know them?" Daryl asked.

Belinda sat back and looked away from him.

"No, I've never seen them in my life," she said

Daryl smiled at her.

"Probably a couple of speed freaks, the way they're acting," Daryl offered.

"Yeah." Belinda smiled and tried to contain her joy. "Probably."

Belinda looked at her watch and sat up.

"I have to get going. You going to stick for the whole show?"

"I guess," he said

"Well, stick around until the opening act is over. Okay?"

Belinda shook his hand.

"See ya later, Daryl," she said.

"Okay, Belinda."

Belinda left.

Daryl turned to the giggling girls. They were gone.

Later, a gentleman in a denim jacket and plaid pants stepped on the stage and grabbed the microphone.

"Good evening," he said. "Please put your drinks down and give your attention to one of the hardest working band of girls on East side. Paw Padds."

As he left the stage, Paw Padds took it. Daryl's insides sunk to the ground. Paw Padds was Belinda and the two giggly freak girls. Belinda grabbed the microphone while her guitar hung from a strap around her shoulder. The rat-nest girl took the drums. The eighties girl stood at the side; a bass strung around her and a microphone by her lips.

Belinda looked up at the crowd. Her eyes found Daryl's. They exchanged smiles.

"Hi, Daryl," Belinda chided. "This one is for you."

The song opened with a mellow bass and creeping cymbal. The guitar slowly dripped in like grained crystal, her hands at the bottom of the guitar's neck and carefully picking away. Belinda started singing out words that Daryl could barely understand. He noticed people in the crowd repeating the words, making it a little clearer for him. Then from out of nowhere, the room exploded. The drums pounded out faster, trying to keep pace with the guitar. Belinda sang slowly, conflicting with the speed of the music. The room jumped and shoved along with the song. Paw Padds connected everyone's pulse and brought the crowd to the edge.

The song finished. Daryl noticed that there was no guitar solos or any kind of chorus. No one seemed to care.

Paw Padds plowed through fourteen songs. Each one was original in sound, never repeating in any note or tune. Belinda switched guitars a few times and often abused them with a cowbell or a screwdriver. For the next hour they had the world at their feet.

* * *

Belinda found him after the set. Daryl looked red. Belinda told him not to worry about it; she was just as bad to string him along.

"You were really killing them out there," Daryl told her.

"Eh," Belinda shrugged. "My second guitar was missing a string. I fucked up the song."

"I don't think anyone really noticed," Daryl said. "I didn't."

Frank Black and his band took the stage and the crowd's attention. He was not as hard or experimental as Paw Padds, but the crowd loved him. Daryl and Belinda moved far from the crowd, avoiding the drunken pit that formed in front of the stage.

When the first song ended, Belinda brought her mouth to his ear.

"Let's go," she screamed.

"Where?" Daryl asked.

"Away."

Belinda smiled at him, making his insides melt. Daryl followed her out.

* * *

Belinda dragged Daryl by the hand across the street to the Half Shell Diner. It was fairly busy. They sat in a booth by the window. They skipped the menu and ordered burgers and fries.

"I fuckin' love fries, you know?" she stated. "I hope you're not mad that I dragged you out of there?"

"No. I'll go anywhere with you." He quickly covered his mouth, turning red again. "I mean..."

"I know what you mean."

"I'm not some groupie who has a hard-on for rock chicks," Daryl explained. "I never heard of you before. Well, that's not altogether true. My editor, Tony, he gave me one of your CDs."

"Have you listened to it yet?"

"No. But he was really going on about you."

"All good things, I hope."

"Oh, well, I can't exactly remember. They were good things, especially about your heart," Daryl said.

"You like it there at Stove Topp?"

"I used to. Now? I know it's good for me. The exposure, you know. But lately, I don't think that it really expresses me. You know?"

"Yeah, kinda like me and the recording," Belinda said. "For so long we tried to get a producer, but all they wanted to do was make us sound like the other people who were making music now. I like Bikini Kill and Liz Phair but is it really honest of me to copy their sound? So, I started producing myself. We just did some sessions on two tracks and mixed it at Wharton Piers. Labels started noticing us. It took us time to find one that was going to let us keep our sound, but we found a good one. Burkel Sound."

"Man, I'm so envious and jealous of you," Daryl said.

"Shut up."

"No one will take what I want to do seriously," Daryl said. "They all think I'm crazy or stupid or something."

"Well, what do you want to do?"

Belinda leaned in, truly curious.

"I wrote this book. It's a kid's book, but adults can read it, too. It's called 'The Michelina's Show.' She's a white cat. It starts when she's born at the cat orphanage. Well, you know how the kitten is supposed to stay with the mother for six months and learn things, that is cat school. So the first half of the book is Michelina going through cat school, then she gets a family and meets the other cats in the neighborhood. She has all of these adventures and learns about human beings and how to manipulate them and stuff. You know, being a cat."

"I love it," she said. "Is it done? Can I read it?"

"Okay. Sure."

"What? Why are you acting weird about it?" she asked. "If you don't want me to read it, I won't."

"You're the first person who ever acted positive. It's a weird feeling."

"What does that tell you?"

Daryl shrugged.

"You have to stop hanging around assholes with their heads up their asses who wouldn't know something good unless someone told them that it was good," Belinda said.

The food came. They ate.

"I have a feeling your book is going to be big," Belinda said. "Look how hard it's been for you. No one wants to take a chance on it. You hate your day job, right?"

"Positively."

"That's a pattern that leads to better things. You'll see."

When they finished eating, Belinda asked, "Do you think you would have time to design our next album cover. Well, it might not be an album, more like an EP. But it won't be for a few months. We're touring down the East Coast for a few months, and then coming back here to record."

"Sure. I'd love to."

"You know, since you know cats so much and our group is called Paw Padds."

"Yeah, okay."

She reached into her back pocket and took out a pad. "Here, write your number down."

He did.

She looked at it and said, "Cool. I have to get going. I'll give you a call."

Belinda stood up and offered her hand. Daryl shook it.

"Good night, Daryl Hersh. It was fun."

He wanted to say: Will you marry me? Can you heal me? Instead, he said, "Bye."

Daryl watched her leave the diner.

* * *

He could not get her out of his mind.

Once Daryl met up with Kate the next day, he told her all about Belinda.

"You are so fuckin' in love," she declared.

"Shut up."

"Did you get her number?"

"Shit, no. My mind was in a complete daze," Daryl said.

"That's what you get for being mesmerized by a pair of tits," Kate said.

"Hey, she is more than just a pair of tits," Daryl corrected. "God, she has the greatest ass."

"You're in love," she chided.

He played the disc that Tony gave him, repeatedly. He stretched out on the floor and surrounded himself with the noise, studying the liner notes on the sleeve, hoping to find some bit of information that would extend her life history to him.

Belinda Kastner, songwriter, guitarist, producer.

That was it.

Daryl then bought their other disc and played it every chance that he had. He even played them at work, repeatedly, annoying his boss and co-workers.

"Give it a rest," they said. "Here put this on instead." They handed him Real McCoy.

At home, there was no one to tell him to turn it off. Daryl played Paw Padds while he worked on the second book of "The Michelina Show."

After a few weeks, he started to feel stupid. He noticed he was becoming a lovesick loser infatuated with a celebrity that he would never see again. But Belinda did say she was going to call when she got back into town. She wanted to work with him. Could she have really meant it? It was not the first time Daryl got empty offers for his work. "Yeah, man. It will be cool," they said. "You do the drawings, and I'll write the words."

Daryl didn't really want to work with her. He wanted to be near her, hold her, and smell her. This was more than a job. He thought about marrying her.

Stupid, he later thought.

Daryl decided to play it cool and keep his options open. If he met another girl during the months Belinda was away, he was not going to let it bother him. Then, if she called, they could do the cover. Daryl planned to let the next few months drop off his back and take the days like a grain of salt.

* * *

It did not go as planned.

* * *

"No, Daryl," Tony said. "It's a great fuckin' book but I'm not printing any of it."

Daryl jumped out of the beanbag chair and placed his hands on the desk.

"Just an excerpt. Just give it a fuckin' try. What could possibly happen? What, you think you're going to lose all of your readers?"

Tony looked Daryl in the eye.

"Yes," Tony said. "I can't risk that. I have to compete with all of those legits out there with all of their big-pocketed advertisers paying them a butt-load of money. Where are my advertisers? Nowhere. I have none. I cannot take any risks because it is me on the line. My zine. Where do you go if it all goes wrong?"

"I'm nowhere now. I'm shit."

"That's not true," Tony whined. "I helped you get recognized on the fuckin' island. There isn't a punk or freak in those clubs who are not familiar with your name or your drawings."

"So you're not going to do it?"

"No. I'm sorry Daryl."

"Fuck."

"You're going to do what I think you're going to do."

"I'm sorry, Tony."

"So am I," he said. "I really liked working with you, but I understand."

* * *

"Fuck him," Kate said.

"That's your response to everything," Daryl said. "Fuck Lisa.

Fuck Tony."

"They can fuck each other," she offered. "Now, there's a scene for porn history."

Kate and Daryl sat in front of the television at his apartment. It was just after midnight, and Dave Kendal was introducing a new video on 120 minutes. Kate had just arrived an hour ago with a heavy gym bag. When Daryl asked what was in it, she told him that it was her work toys. Daryl quickly shrunk away from the bag and offered her a drink.

They did not talk much. Daryl grew sleepy, trying to stay awake.

"Maybe you should get going."

"Why?" Kate asked.

"I'm tired."

"After 120 Minutes, okay" Kate pleaded. "You know how much I like English guys."

Daryl was too tired to argue.

Kate kept stealing glances at him. Daryl's eyes opened, then closed, then opened again. She smiled. It was the cutest sight.

Daryl finally fell asleep.

* * *

Daryl woke up in the same spot on the couch. Kate stood with a video camera pointed at him. The red recording light blinked.

"What are you doing?" he asked.

Kate stopped the camera and moved it away from her face.

"Daryl, is that you?" she asked.

He stood up.

"Yeah, it's me," he said. "Who the fuck else would I be - an alien invader."

"It's just..."

"What were you doing with the camera?" he asked, walking to the kitchen.

"Well...I...You see..."

He stopped at the refrigerator and realized something. "Were you just recording me sleeping?"

"Uh, heh, heh, yes."

"Oh, man."

"Are you mad?"

He was, but he was also tired.

"Just leave," he said.

"Daryl, I'm sorry..."

"What the fuck were you thinking? What the fuck is the matter with you?"

"What?"

"You know how personal this is for me. Were you going to sell it or something?"

"No. It wasn't that juicy," she said.

"Give me the tape."

"No."

"Yes."

"Listen, Daryl, this is important, okay. You're not just any sleepwalker. You're doing things with these Beings. In a way, it's fuckin' amazing, but it is not normal. I met a guy who studies ghosts and hallucinations and shit, and I told him all about you. He's legit. He's a doctor at N.Y.U. and he's really interested in you."

"I can't believe you did this."

Kate stepped closer to Daryl and took his hand. She said, "Daryl, whether you like it or not, you are special. You should have seen yourself. You looked so happy and so loved. Why do they make you feel like that?"

"I don't know," Daryl offered.

"Let me take the tape. You don't have to meet him if you don't want to, but let him look at it."

"Okay."

* * *

One of the regular shoplifters came in around 2 P.M. Daryl, blistering CDs at the back of the store, recognized him right away. Every week, once a week, the thief entered the store with a bulky bag and then left the store without buying anything. Every time the thief left, he set off the alarm, ignored it, and disappeared on the street. What good was an alarm if it turns on after the fact, Daryl always thought?

The short and greasy thief held a store bag stuffed with CDs and walked over to the register. The thief talked to the cashier. His name was Dave and he didn't speak English very well since he came to the states a year ago from South Africa. Nevertheless, Dave knew a shit load about American top 40 and proved to be a great help.

The thief grew angry. Dave kept his hands up in an apologetic fashion and spoke in a calm voice. Dave then made eye contact with Daryl, arching his brows in a plea of help.

"What's going on, Dave?" Daryl asked, coming around to Dave's side. Big smile.

"I'll tell you what's going on," the thief said. "The other day my mom bought me these ÇDs for my birthday, but I have these already. I'd like to return them. I have a receipt and I'd like my damn money back."

Daryl took his time and looked at the merchandise. They were fine; he just wanted to look professional. He then inspected the receipt. It looked like it was used to wash and dry dishes then attached back together with Scotch tape. In fact, there was piece of tape right over the spot that said the customer paid cash. The word 'cash' was graphed on the paper. Daryl saw too many of them; it was fake.

"You want almost $300 back," Daryl stated.

"So it seems," the thief said. "My mama really loves me, but she doesn't know me."

"Not like us," Daryl said under his breath.

"What does that mean?"

"Nothing. I didn't say anything."

"Yes, you did. You said, 'Not like us.' What? You sayin' you know me?"

"No."

"Dumb ass."

"Excuse me, I'm going to have to ask you to leave," Daryl said.

"The fuck you will!"

All the customers turned to the scene.

Daryl cracked a reluctant smile at them.

"Listen..."

"No, you listen. I don't know what the fuck is going on here. I buy music from this store all the time, and I never had a problem. Now that I want to return something you treat me like a common fuckin' criminal."

"You are a criminal, asshole," Daryl said. "You've been stealing from us for months, and now you come in with this fake receipt and expect me to give you hundreds in cash. Fuck you."

"No, fuck you, you little faggot ass cock sucker."

The thief grabbed Daryl from across the counter and pulled him out by his shirt.

* * *

"You always hated that job, anyway," Kate said.

Daryl and Kate lay on his bed. Daryl pressed an ice pack to his eye where the thief punched him. His stomach was achy from the kicks, but his bruised jaw felt better.

"It's good that you quit," she assured him.

"Yeah, but now I'm not so sure," Daryl said. "I don't have much in my savings."

"Unemployment."

"Maybe."

"You'll find something, sweetie."

"Uh, huh."

"Well, here is some good news: you remember that tape I made a couple of weeks ago?"

"Yeah, what did your doctor friend have to say about it?"

"He pretty much said it was an excuse to see me without paying, and he had no real interest in you."

"He was a customer?"

"Not anymore," Kate said. "What a dick. I'm sorry."

"Don't worry about it," Daryl said. "I'm kind of glad it didn't work out."

They laid there quietly until...

"How do you do it?"

"What do you mean?" Kate asked.

"How do you make yourself be with so many guys at night?"

"It's not like you think. I don't have sex with them in any way, and I don't let them see me naked. It's safe."

"I guess."

"What does that mean?"

"Nothing. I don't want you to think I'm looking down on you. I'm not."

"Okay," she urged. "Say what you have to say."

"It's intimate, you know. I just don't know how you can be intimate with so many different guys," Daryl said. "You're someone who should be treasured, you know. Kept to one."

"You're so sweet," Kate gushed.

She moved closer and hugged Daryl.

"Stop," he whined.

"Can I tell you a secret?"

"Yeah," Daryl said.

"I haven't had sex in three years."

"No."

"True."

"Why?"

"Because I'm waiting for you, or someone like you," Kate said.

"Oh."

She looked at him. Daryl tried to shy his eyes away from her, but he could not stop looking at them. Their heads moved closer and they kissed. Just as they were going to fall in deep, Daryl and Kate stopped and looked at each other. They laughed and settled down. Kate and Daryl spent the night together, sleeping.

* * *

The next few weeks, Daryl toured around the city and filled out applications at retail stores. The most popular response: We are not hiring right now, especially for management. Although, Letchers, a kitchen supply store, offered him a position but only as a cashier for minimum wage. They never hired managers off the street, too many loss prevention issues.

The other half of his days, Daryl wrote and drew. He went through his old short stories and shaped them up for submission to magazines. In the back of his mind, he knew that he was not going to hear from them for months and they might not even buy them, but he tried, keeping his mind occupied, hoping that they would sell for a penny a word.

At night, he spent most of his time reading. He read all 10 of his Ellen West's books for the 24th time. She was the only author Daryl reread continuously. Daryl read other authors a few times before, but not as many times as her books. He loved the writing style and had been reading her books since he was a teen-ager.

Daryl hung out with Kate a few times a week. Lately, she worked more hours. When he did see her, she was shot and tired, and she always had a few extra bucks to give Daryl. He pushed it away at first, but then Kate made a face at him, telling him how hard she worked for it, how hard she worked for him so that he could eat, then he accepted it.

The first time they hung out after the kiss, there was no weirdness. They had kissed before and felt just as silly about it. They learned to move on and kept their friendship the same.

Daryl never stopped thinking about Belinda Kastner. He continued to play nothing but the Paw Padds CDs. He knew all the words and unconsciously tapped a limb to the drumbeats. He paged through the Aquarian and The Voice and scanned for tour dates, trying to figure out where she was and when she was coming back to town. Daryl knew how stupid and obsessive he was being, but he could not stop himself. Belinda dominated his mind.

Time ganged up on him. Daryl had too much of it; too much time to think. He wondered about his parents and who they were. Why did they leave him on the train? Was it because they knew he was broken? Was it because of the Beings who hovered over him in his sleep? He was only ten years old; at least, that was how the social worker aged him. Daryl could be a few years older or younger. It was a small detail, but Daryl thought it was a major one.

When Daryl was 19 he went to the library and performed his own investigation since he had no money of his own to buy a detective. He searched through all the phone books of the towns that the train passed through, starting from 1985, scanning names and addresses, hoping something would break through his amnesia. Daryl gave up after eight phone books and realized he was being obsessive.

Just like now.

Daryl knew that Belinda was someone special. Belinda was going to change his life. Then again, this was all in his mind. He had two conversations with the girl. Could he honestly destine his life with her under those conditions?

* * *

It had been two weeks since he last saw Kate. They talked on the phone a few times, but the conversations were short. Kate sounded tired and sad. He tried to get her to meet him, but she blew him off and made Daryl promise not to surprise her and show up on her doorstep. She wanted to be alone. Kate told him that she was going through something that she needed to figure out by herself. Daryl promised to give her some time but he was not going to wait long.

Daryl grew tired of waiting and was ready for the consequences. Using the key Kate gave him years ago, he entered the building and walked up to her apartment. He banged on the door and called out her name. Getting no response, Daryl looked at his watch. It was almost 2 P.M. She was usually awake at that hour. He knocked again.

"Kate. It's me, Daryl."

He slipped the key in the lock and opened the door. Daryl stepped inside and looked around. It was the usual mess: hundreds of videos surrounded the television, piles of books mounted the floor, canvases and paints covered the couch. Daryl checked the open kitchen. Nothing. He opened the door to the bedroom. The bed looked slept in, but no Kate. He walked across the room and opened the door to the bathroom.

Daryl found her.

Kate was naked with red-tinted bath water wrinkling her skin in the bathtub. Her eyes were closed with the most peaceful expression on her face. Daryl stepped closer and saw her hands resting on her stomach. One wrist was gently slit open while she held the razor in the other hand.

Daryl felt dizzy like he was falling into an abyss. He landed on his knees. He could not take his eyes off her. Daryl cried for an hour, then he called for the police.

* * *

After the investigation, the police concluded that it was suicide. Although there was no note, there was also no sign of struggle, forced entry, or other wounds on Kate's body. Daryl did not argue with the conclusion, but Kate's parents in Bayonne, N.J. did. They did not accept suicide too well since they were die-hard Catholics. If they accepted it, then they had to accept that their daughter was in hell and that she damned them to go there as well because of her actions.

Daryl disbelieved that theory. Kate was the sweetest and kindest person he knew. Hell had no use for her. It was God's benefit to get her so early. But Daryl still felt cheated and angry. He missed her. She was his best friend. Now, he was alone. He was so afraid to go out in the world and make friends. Daryl had a love/hate relationship with humans. In some ways, he wanted to be around them because he could not stand being with himself, but in other ways, he could not stand being with human arrogance and selfishness.

Kate's mother called Daryl up a few weeks after the funeral and told him that they were done going through their daughter's stuff. He could drop by Kate's apartment and take whatever he wanted. By the end of the month, the landlord had to make the apartment available for the new tenants.

Daryl rented a van and spent a day there. He went through all of Kate's canvases and sketchpads. Daryl had a hard time deciding on what to keep and what to throw out; even the unfinished works impressed him. In the end, he kept 90 percent of her work.

The video collection was a lot simpler. Daryl never had the heart to tell Kate how much he hated her taste in movies. He found them juvenile. But, Daryl thought, if he was a teen-ager, he would have loved all that gore and bouncing flesh running around in mellow-drama. He kept ten videos that Kate always talked about; ten that he felt represented what he loved about her.

He also took the video that Kate shot of him sleepwalking. It was labeled Daryl Sleepwalking. Daryl packed it up with the others and brought it home.

* * *

Drew.

Wrote.

Ate.

Shit.

Pissed.

Ejaculated.

Time flew by and stayed the same.

Daryl kept to his apartment for weeks. If he ran out of food, he had it delivered. He only left his apartment to drop off the rent check and open his mailbox. Daryl mostly received junk mail and bills. He paid the bills, but his savings was shrinking.

He did not talk to anyone. The phone never rang with the prospect of a job or a human he once knew to check in on him to see how he was doing. It seemed like Daryl was forgotten by the world and left with himself.

He hated himself.

At times, it was not that bad.

Every night the Beings watched him. They made him laugh and

kept Daryl active. They came by more often than before, as if they knew he needed the company. Daryl woke up in different places of the apartment: bathtub, front door, under the bed, etc. As grateful as he was for their company, he still craved human contact.

His first thought was to call Kate, then he realized he could not. Liz often popped into his head, urging him to call her. He could not remember her number so he looked it up in his phone book. When his eyes saw the hand written digits in the book, the number came back to him. Stupid you, Daryl thought.

Daryl sat on the floor with his back on the couch. He dialed the number. It picked up after three rings.

"Hello." It was Jeanie.

"Is Liz there?"

"Excuse me," she whined. "You'll have to talk English."

Daryl cleared his throat.

"Sorry," he said. "Is Liz there?"

"No. You want me to take a message?"

"Will she be in later?"

"Who is this?"

"I'll just drop by later."

"Daryl, is that you?" Jeanie turned even more obnoxious, superior, and intimidating. "Liz doesn't want to see you. Okay?"

"You don't know that," he protested.

"I don't? She told me she's scared of you. You're a psycho, all right. No one with your condition can be right in the head."

"You're the one who put that shit in her head," Daryl stated. "I would never kill anyone."

"Oh, yeah. Like you or anyone else would admit to murder."

Jeanie hung up.

Pissed, Daryl threw the phone across the floor. He felt like doing some serious crying, but nothing came out.

* * *

Daryl gathered himself together and took a shower. He dressed in his best clothes: suit, tie, pants, and shoes. He looked completely non-threatening; like he was going to spread the good Lord's message.

He left the apartment at 6 P.M., picked up some flowers, and walked to Liz's. He was determined to talk to her, get her to change her view of him.

Daryl rang the buzzer at Liz's building.

"Yes." It was Liz.

Daryl straightened up as if she was in front of him.

"Hi," he said. "It's me."

"What do you want Daryl?"

"I just wanted to see you. To see how you're doing. "It's been a while."

"I'm fine. Now, please go away."

Daryl moved his mouth closer to the speaker, leaning against the door.

"Please, Liz, just talk to me. I need to talk to you. I'm not looking to get back together with you. I just want you in my life. I really need someone in my life that I can...shit, interact or something. I feel like...I'm dead. I'm surrounded by ghosts and alone. Please, just talk to me."

There was no answer. Liz probably took her finger off the "Listen" button a long time ago, he thought. Daryl gave her another few minutes.

Nothing.

Daryl dropped the flowers by the door and went home.

* * *

All the lights were off. The blinds were down. Darkness. Night? Day? Daryl was not sure when he woke up on the kitchen table. He sat up and walked to the living room. Daryl dropped on the couch and noticed the answering machine blinking. He had a message. He did not remember the phone ringing. Probably a telemarketer, he thought.

He pressed the "Play" button.

"Hi, Daryl. It's Belinda. We just got back a week ago. Sorry, I didn't get back to you sooner. Crazy time. So give me a call so we can make plans about the EP cover. My number is 212-555-1213. Bye."

Belinda had been back a week when she called? When did she call? Holy shit, Daryl thought.

Daryl played the message again and wrote down her number. He went to the bathroom, took a shower, brushed his teeth, then, in fresh clothes, sat back on the couch, calm and composed, he dialed her number.

The line connected on the seventh ring.

"Hello?" Belinda sounded sleepy, groggy.

"Hi. It's Daryl."

"Oh, hi."

"I'm sorry I didn't get back to you sooner. I was, uh, away and I just got your message," Daryl explained.

"You just got home now?"

"Yeah. Why?"

"It's almost 2 A.M.," she said with a laugh.

"Oh, shit. Is it?" Daryl stood up and paced the couch. "I'm sorry."

"What are you doing tomorrow?" Belinda asked.

"Nothing. My schedule is free."

"Wanna meet me at Greeko's at 1. Christopher and Second."

"Okay. Great," Daryl said. "Again, I'm sorry about calling so late."

She hummed the sweetest sound.

"It's okay," Belinda sighed. "I'm glad you called tonight."

Belinda hung up.

Daryl flipped.

* * *

Daryl arrived a half hour early and sat with his portfolio next to him at the booth. He brought his best sketches and a copy of "The Michelina Show." He drank three glasses of water and nervously jiggled his leg. At five to one, he went to pee. When Daryl exited the bathroom, Belinda walked in. She spotted him and smiled, taking off her sunglasses. Belinda walked up to Daryl and offered her hand.

"Hey, been waiting long?" she asked.

"No. I just got here."

He took her hand. It felt warm and soft. He loved it. He wanted to pull her close and hug her, but decided against it, avoiding a psycho impression.

They sat.

After the waitress took their orders, Daryl motioned to his portfolio. "Would you like to look at them now before the food comes?"

"Yeah, good idea," Belinda said.

Daryl opened the portfolio in front of her. She quietly flipped through the protected images, glancing at each one.

Daryl studied her face. It was small and cat-like with the lightest freckles peaking out of the milkiest skin. He was dying for her.

"Well, there really is no need for this," Belinda said. She closed the portfolio and handed it to him. "I want you to do this. You don't have to sell me."

"Oh, I just thought...you know, to make sure you're sure."

"I'm sure," she smiled.

"Okay," Daryl sighed.

"So, just give me a good selection and I'll take them back to the girls," Belinda said.

"Next week okay?"

"Fine."

"Good."

"Well, now that that is out of the way," she said. "How have you been?"

"Oh, okay," Daryl said.

"Liar," she said. "What happened?"

"Well, I got beat up, dumped, rejected, quit my job, and my best friend died," Daryl said. "Not in that order, mind you."

"Not that girl from the other night?"

"Yeah. Kate."

"I'm so sorry."

Belinda took his hand. It triggered a release deep in Daryl but he held it back, not wanting to cry in front of her."

"She killed herself. It's fucked up," Daryl said. "I thought I knew her. I did know her. I knew she was sad and disappointed. I saw it, but..."

"It's not your fault, Daryl."

He believed her, making his heart squishy.

The food arrived, and they ate.

"You from New York?" Belinda asked.

"I'm not sure," Daryl said. "I moved here when I was eighteen to go to college. Before that I was at an orphanage in Ontario."

"An orphan? Interesting."

"Yep."

"So you don't know who your parents are."

"Yeah, but it's not from lack of trying. Plus, I have a bad case of amnesia since I was ten years old."

"You mean, you can't remember even now?"

"Yep," he clarified.

"That sucks."

He smiled.

"It's not so bad," he said. "Not getting people to pick you for adoption was a lot worse. But here I am. A survivor, I guess. How about you?"

"Well, I came here from Buffalo when I was eighteen. Went to college and got a degree in journalism. I actually had a good job lined up at a major paper but I backed out."

"Which paper?"

"I'd rather not say. It was big and whenever I tell people they tell me how stupid I was for turning it down."

"So it was a stupid move."

"Exactly what my parents said. So here I am almost two years later. Sad, huh."

"You're not doing so bad. Your band is getting great word of mouth. You're getting attention. You'll strike gold eventually."

She threw her hand at him.

"Ahh, you're just saying the same thing I told you the other night," she said. "Oh, did you bring that book?"

Daryl handed it to her. Belinda flipped through the pages and smiled at the drawings.

"Oh, these cats are so cute," she gushed.

"Not too cute for Paw Padds."

"I'm sure you'll draw something that fits our sound."

Belinda winked at him.

Daryl fell deeper.

* * *

Daryl drew twenty pictures in two days. He called up Belinda and asked when he could show them to her.

"Damn, you're fast," she exclaimed.

"All I have is time," he said.

"We're sort of rehearsing at my apartment. Why don't you swing on by tonight?"

"Sort of rehearsing?"

"Well, we can't plug in the instruments because the neighbors complain, so we rehearse unplugged. Seven o'clock okay?"

"Cool," Daryl said. "Where do you live?"

* * *

The apartment was on 8th Ave between 28th and 29th Street. The first thing Daryl noticed was the low lighting of the street. She is a brave girl, he thought.

They buzzed him in. Daryl entered the elevator, pulled the heavy cage door shut, and went up. When the cables strained, Daryl grabbed the wall and feared the worst.

Belinda waited for him on the 3rd floor. She wore red flannel pajamas and untied combat boots. She smiled at his fear clinging to the walls of the elevator.

"Hi," she said.

"Hey."

She opened the door and said, "Don't worry, it's perfectly safe."

Daryl composed himself and released the wall.

"Oh, you thought I was scared of the elevator. No. No. I was just...uh...scared that I might..."

"Uh, huh." Belinda closed the door behind him.

They moved down the hall.

The apartment was a warehouse space converted into a studio. Pipes lined the ceiling and weaved in and out of the floor and walls. The back corners of the room were walled off to form bedrooms. Guitars and drums locked up in their cases sat next to some recording and sound equipment. Just next to the kitchen area was a couple of couches where the eighties girl and rat-haired girl sat. They smiled wide and said, "Daryl," in unison.

Daryl waved to them, shy.

Belinda locked the apartment door and offered Daryl a spot on the couch. With his portfolio between his legs, he sat next to the eighties girl. She took her hand off the bass on her lap and offered it for a shake. "Hi, I'm Jess," she said. Jess pointed to the other girl. "She's Prudee."

"Hey," Prudee said.

Belinda handed Daryl a beer.

"How are ya doing?" Daryl asked, completely nervous. "So you wanna see what I got?"

The three young women smiled and catcalled.

"Ooo, take it out, cutie," Jess said.

Daryl, catching on to their perverted subtext, blushed and opened his portfolio, nodding his head and smiling. He divided the pictures in three piles and passed them around. Awes and ohs slipped out of the girl's mouths as they looked through them. At first they seemed kind of mocking, but then they turned serious. Daryl felt proud.

"I tried to make an even amount of cute and nasty pictures," Daryl offered.

"I like this one," Belinda said. It was a cat version of the band playing live.

Prudee and Jess agreed.

"Jesus, you only met us once," Jess said. "How could you

remember what we look like from one night?"

Daryl shrugged his shoulders. He honestly did not know.

"You're right, Belinda," Prudee said. "He's a genius."

Daryl looked at Belinda. She blushed.

"I told them about your book," Belinda said.

"You read it. Wow."

"I finished it that night. I couldn't put it down."

"Thanks," Daryl said.

They looked at each other. There were no smiles or jokes. Their gazes were serious. Belinda bit her lower lip and stole a quick scan of Daryl's body. Daryl felt a stir down below.

"Well," Daryl said, "if you really like the one of the group, I can make some individual ones for the sleeve."

"You mean, like, instead of our pictures?" Jess asked.

"Yeah, if you want."

The girls said, "Cool."

* * *

Daryl sat on the couch and watched the band rehearse a few new songs that Belinda wrote. She was patient with Jess and Prudee, showing them and reciting with her mouth how the song sounded in her head. Daryl watched Belinda. He could not keep his eyes off her, and she knew it. When Belinda caught him looking at her a few times, she just smiled. Belinda liked his attention and the fact that Daryl blushed every time she caught him.

After a couple of hours, Prudee announced that she was tired and wanted to go to bed. Since she shared the apartment with Belinda, Prudee did not have to go too far. She gave Daryl a sly wink on the way to her bedroom.

Jess, getting the plan, packed up her bass. She lived a few blocks away. Jess thanked Daryl for his work and mussed his hair.

They were alone.

It was quiet.

Too quiet.

"Maybe I should get going, too," Daryl said.

"You don't have to," Belinda said. "I mean I don't mind the company."

"Okay," Daryl said.

Belinda sat down next to him on the couch and tucked her leg under her butt. She faced Daryl's profile, giving him her attention. Belinda smiled. Daryl smiled back, not knowing what he was supposed to do. Belinda laughed.

"What?" he asked.

"Nothing. You're cute."

"Oh."

"You know, I haven't been completely honest with you," she said.

"What do you mean?"

"I've met you before that night at the club."

"Really."

"Yeah. I've been in The Shiny Disc many times."

"Oh. Jesus, I can't honestly say that I remember you there."

"This might sound stupid, but even back then I thought you were cute."

"Oh."

Daryl felt a little dizzy.

"I guess you could say I had a crush on you," Belinda said. "It wasn't until I found out that you were 'thee' Daryl Hersh from Stove Topp that I got the nerve to approach you. Stupid, huh?"

"What do you mean?"

"Ever since that night, I couldn't stop thinking about you. I was scared that I would never see you again. Now, that is stupid."

"No, it's not. I felt the same way."

They looked at each other and felt weightless. Like magnets, they moved their heads together and lightly joined their lips, tasting. Their bodies moved closer. Their arms wrapped around each other, careful of what parts they touched. When the tips of their tongues connected...

"Woo! Woo!" Prudee screamed.

They broke apart and laughed. They turned to Prudee's bedroom to see the door closed.

"How did she know? Daryl asked.

"She's a freak."

* * *

For the next month, Belinda and Daryl saw each other almost every night. Most of the time they stayed in and watched T.V., rented videos, or just talked about anything and nothing. They hardly ever fought, often being patient with one another.

"9 o'clock," Belinda declared at his apartment.

"What's on?" Daryl asked.

"My Daughter And Her Secret Affair With My Husband," she said, changing the channel.

"You put on Lifetime. It's on Lifetime?"

"Yeah, so."

"I hate the movies on that channel."

"I've been waiting to see this movie all week."

Belinda gave Daryl the saddest look.

"Oh, crap," he said.

They watched the movie.

Belinda also bended to Daryl's taste in entertainment.

"Oh, what did you bring?" she asked as he entered her apartment.

"A classic. It's television movie. But not just any television movie, it also appeared on the big screen because of its popularity," Daryl said.

She took the tape out of the bag.

"Battlestar Galactica? Crap."

"What? It's a classic."

"Classic crap. I don't want to watch a sci-fi movie."

"It's not just a sci-fi movie. It is the meaning of life. Beside, you owe me for that incest movie we watched the other night."

Belinda stuck her tongue out and took the tape to the VCR.

Belinda started production on the EP. They recorded mostly at night when the rates were cheaper. Daryl hung out with them a few nights, often falling asleep on the couch in the recording room. It went well, but there were times when they had to rehearse a song twenty times and the band was still not able to get it right. It frustrated Belinda to high heaven. Prudee and Jess kept their mouths shut, fighting not to tell her off.

It wasn't until the band took a break that the tension and frustration erupted. Prudee accidentally knocked over Belinda's Gibson.

"Jesus, couldn't you just call me an evil cunt," Belinda said. "You didn't have to attack my guitar."

"I swear to fuckin' God. I didn't do it on purpose," Prudee said.

Belinda strummed the guitar to see if it was okay. She then played some of the stunted song. It was out of tune, but it created the sound she desired.

"Prudee, I love you," Belinda gushed.

"What a freak," Jess exclaimed.

Daryl searched for a job. It took a few weeks but he landed a glorious position at Java Joe Joe. He learned to make over twenty different kinds of coffee and espresso drinks and, like any job he acquired, he mastered it in a week. Considering his financial situation, he didn't mind so much. It paid two dollars less than The Disc, and he had Belinda to look forward to at the end of the shift.

Daryl was falling in love with Belinda, and it was completely healthy. He spent any cash he could on her.

"Roses! You dick, you shouldn't have," Belinda said.

"How did you know I wanted this Bon Jovi disc? Daryl, you're spoiling me."

He did not care. Belinda deserved it for the way she made him feel. Daryl was truly happy.

* * *

The snag arrived about a month and a half into the relationship. Daryl and Belinda lay in her bed, naked, tired, satisfied. It was just after 1 A.M. Daryl started to get out of bed.

"Where are ya going?" Belinda asked.

"Home," Daryl said.

"Stay tonight."

"I shouldn't."

"I don't snore."

"Yes, you do. I heard you. But that's not it," he assured her.

"Do I smell?"

"Besides like a sex kitten, no."

"Let me guess," she said. "It's not me, but you."

"It is me," Daryl said.

He turned away from her. He released a depressed sigh.

Belinda moved up behind Daryl and hugged him, pressing her chin into his shoulder.

"Tell me," she said. "I'm falling so in love with you. Please, tell me."

Belinda's words cut him deep, making Daryl feel hollow.

"I'm falling in love with you, too," he said. "That's why it's so hard."

"Tell me."

"I sleepwalk," he said.

"That's it?" Belinda asked.

"No. I see...Beings in my sleep."

"Beings?"

"I'm not sure who or what they are. I call them Beings. They stand around me in my sleep and watch over me."

"Okay," Belinda said.

"Should I leave?"

"Why?"

"You're not scared of me, of them?"

"No," she said. "I'm not going to let that be the reason why I can't see that ugly face of yours in the morning."

Daryl released a sigh of relief and smiled.

"I love you," he said.

They celebrated in bed.

* * *

Daryl was getting ready for work. He was half dressed in his Java Joe Joe uniform when the phone rang. Daryl thought not to answer it. The time was about 1 P.M., and he knew that Belinda was mixing until 4 P.M. Belinda never took breaks during a mix.

But still...

"Hello," Daryl said into the phone.

"Daryl Hersh, please."

"This is."

"Great. I wasn't sure I was going to get ya," the man on the phone said. "You can never be sure that this time of day that you can always find a person there. I mean it's almost 1 P.M. What are the chances, right? Did you think you would be home? But then again, I don't know your life. You could be home everyday at this time. That means you don't have a 9 to 5 job. So you must be in something retail related. So if I called yesterday you might not have been home."

"Um, who are you?" Daryl interrupted.

"Oh, I'm sorry. My name is Tom Cualos," he said. "I'm an editor at Maddox Publishing. We're sort of a sister company with Sporadic House Publishing. Actually it is more sister than you think. My boss is actually the sister of the president of Sporadic House Publishing. Weird, huh."

"Oh, shit."

"Yeah, you're probably getting the right idea. I didn't call to tell you that I hated your book and we're not interested in publishing it."

* * *

As soon as he got off the phone, Daryl called work and told them that there was a family emergency and he would not be able to make it for a few hours.

Dressed and ready, Daryl ran to the studio where Paw Padds mixed. He entered the room and saw that they were joined by a short, hairy guy smoking a clove cigarette. They all looked at him. Daryl stood there, panting and happy like a fiend.

"Daryl, are you alright?" Belinda asked.

Daryl coughed, trying to form words.

"Man, is he, like, on something," asked the clove smoker sitting at the control board.

Belinda ignored him and stepped up to Daryl.

"What is it?" she asked.

"Ma ma ma."

"His Mom!" offered clove smoker.

Belinda turned to him with a pissed off look on her face. "Pablo, would you shut up, please."

Pablo, the clove smoker, held up his hands in surrender.

Belinda softened up and turned back to Daryl.

"Maddox Pub...Publisher," Daryl said.

"Yeah?"

"Pub...pub..."

"They're going to publish your book," Pablo declared.

Belinda shot Pablo a wide-eyed look.

Prudee threw an empty coffee cup at Pablo, hitting his head.

"Thank you," Belinda said.

"De nada," Prudee responded.

"That's it," Daryl said.

"They're going to publish your book?" Belinda asked.

"Yes."

They all screamed.

Belinda hugged Daryl, throwing herself at him and pressing his body to the wall. They fell to the floor and laughed.

"Looks like someone owes me an apology," Pablo said to Prudee.

Prudee threw another empty cup at him.

"Owe," Pablo said.

III

Mania
(2001)

Belinda Hersh slept next to Daryl Hersh. It was late at night. She was dressed in her usual cat pajamas with the holes in the crotch and the knees. Daryl called them her porn star pajamas. Belinda smiled and gave him suggestive glances. "You only have yourself to blame," she told him.

She woke up from a slight tremor in the bed. Belinda turned to Daryl and found him doing his thing. He laughed and waved his arms around. Daryl's eyes were open but he saw something Belinda did not see.

Daryl scrunched his face and then looked at his shirt. He left the bed and walked to the closet. Belinda watched him change his white and very clean T-shirt for a new lighter brown one. Daryl walked back to the bed and went to sleep.

Belinda, thinking nothing of what just happened, did the same.

* * *

Belinda was not like the other girls who grew up in Buffalo, New York. Belinda had no idea what she wanted to be when she grew up, and she did not define herself by the kind of man she kept. She never really had friends; they were more like acquaintances. Belinda decided this by the fact that no one ever asked her to hang out or called her when she was sick to find out how she was doing. But that was fine because she had more important things to do.

Belinda spent her early teens listening to music. She had a deep love for Cock Rock: Bon Jovi, Van Halen, Skid Row, and Nelson. She loved the long hair, the dangerous looks, and the power they held between their legs: the guitar. But in some way she felt inadequate.

Belinda wanted to play the guitar but she was not sure she could. She once read an interview with a well-known Cock Rocker who said, "There are no great female guitarists because it is not in their genetic makeup. A guitarist penetrates. Women can't penetrate."

Belinda decided to prove the quote wrong.

She went to her father and asked him if she could get a guitar. Belinda's father was an accountant and had no creative sensibilities at all. In some way, Belinda was nervous about asking him because she felt he would say that it was not practical.

"Wouldn't you rather play the flute?"

"No, I think I want to play the guitar," Belinda assured him.

"I see. I'll discuss this with your mother."

He smiled and nodded at her.

Mom was a self-declared part-time homemaker and a home business owner. From her kitchen, she sold homemade cat magnets. With cheap sewing materials and magnets from the Craft Shop, she spent her days filling orders. Belinda was always impressed with that aspect of her mother; so was her father. Mom raked in about $25,000 a year. Belinda figured that she inherited her creative desire from her mother, so maybe her chances of getting a guitar were good.

Months went by, and Belinda's sixteenth birthday came around. There was a sweet sixteen party, mostly because her mother really wanted it. The party consisted of family.

"Aren't there any friends you want to invite from school," mom asked her.

"No," Belinda stated plainly.

Mom smiled. "Okay."

They celebrated at a local Italian restaurant where Belinda collected cash and clothes, but the biggest prize came from her parents.

"Holy shit, a Fender guitar," she screamed.

"Belinda!" Mom warned, looking around in embarrassment.

"There's an amplifier in there too," her father pointed out.

"I love it. Thank you."

No one saw her after that. Belinda locked herself in her room and she taught herself how to play the guitar with how-to books she stole from the mall bookstore. Belinda practiced discipline. In a few weeks, she moved onto her favorite songs.

In the back of her mind, Belinda felt a bit lonely. She was the only female rock musician in her school and the only one that took music seriously. The loneliness disappeared when she went to N.Y.U. Belinda picked her friends carefully. She disliked many musicians. They were so full of themselves and mostly men. They seemed to consider her a serious fuck just by looking at her, but Belinda was not interested in letting them find out.

Belinda majored in journalism. She thought the major was okay and she seemed to be good at it. Her parents felt proud of her, hoping she would work for the New York Times and get a Pulitzer. But Belinda took music more seriously. While her friends experimented with their bodies and activities, Belinda experimented with her music. She had five guitars, used and abused. She discovered bands like Sonic Youth and The Swirlies. Belinda still loved Cock Rock, but new bands opened new doors for her, extending her.

In her last year of school, Belinda met Prudee and Jess. They were musicians, they were girls, they did not take themselves seriously in an ego way, they were perfect. Belinda formed a band with them. She showed them the songs she wrote, and they immediately knew what she was going for musically. They loved it. Jess and Prudee were happy playing bass and drum. They had no desire to write songs. They just loved to play.

After a month of wordplay, Paw Padds was born. Their name had nothing to do with cats, not in the traditional sense.

* * *

Belinda woke up the next morning, not to the sound of the alarm, but to the touch of Daryl's hand. It moved under her top and gently cupped her left breast. Belinda kept her eyes closed and turned to him. Their lips met and their tongues swirled. He was hard. She was wet. They got down to business like they did every other morning.

* * *

One hour later, Belinda left the bed and took a shower, getting ready for her day. She put on a Posies T-shirt, a blue flannel shirt, and black jeans. She looked at her 27-year-old self in the mirror, fixed her short multi-colored hair with her hand, and decided she was set for the day.

Belinda, Jess, and Prudee were at the last day of mixing their fifth album. Belinda was pretty excited about it; more excited than the last album. This time the label focused on the quintet of singing children that they recently signed instead of Paw Padds. Before, on the fourth album, she created the same sound they made on their third breakthrough album "The Litter Box" to satisfy the pressure of the label.

Now, the press focused on other bands. The real fans showed their devotion in shows and in moderate record sales. There was not as much pressure. Paw Padds stuck to the basics for the new album, and tentatively called it "Hair Ball." They did three takes and stuck with their own instruments. There were no outside musicians. Although, Belinda liked the extra strings and horns on the other albums, this time she wanted something primitive.

In the kitchen, she found Daryl fixing breakfast. He made her a ketchup omelet. His back was to her and his ass shook to a song in his head. Belinda thought he was so cute and showed her affection by grabbing his ass.

"Morning," she said.

"Morning, wild woman," he replied.

They had been married for three years. Daryl proposed when Belinda was about to leave on her first world tour. She immediately said yes, but she worried about when they could make plans for the wedding since she was going to be out of town for so long. Daryl assured Belinda that when she came back to New York she would be ready to marry him.

With the help of Belinda's mom, Daryl planned the wedding, picked out three dresses for Belinda to choose from, and made honeymoon plans based on her tour. Belinda could not believe how hard he worked, and how lucky she felt.

Belinda sat at the kitchen table while he placed the omelet in front of her. Daryl snuck a kiss on her cheek. She smiled at him, remembering their morning ritual.

Daryl prepared a bowl of cereal, Coa Coa Snapps, and sat across from her. He noticed his T-shirt and looked at it, confused.

"Did I go to bed in this?" Daryl asked.

"Nope."

"Oh."

Belinda studied his face. Daryl was remembering. He usually did in the morning.

"They dropped this gunk on me," he said. "Anyway..."

"What time is your interview?" Belinda asked.

"Oh, shit, that's right," Daryl said. "I almost forgot."

"I guess, I should stop fucking your brains out."

"Please, don't. It's the highlight of my day," he said. "Not these stupid interviews."

"Comic Page. You don't want to piss them off," she offered.

"Please, they should consider themselves lucky to get an interview with me, not to sound too conceited."

Ever since the second book of The Michelina's Show made the Bestseller's list, Daryl became the focus of the media, but not for his writing. They were more interested in his amnesia. It could have been worse; they could have found out about his Beings and his sleepwalking.

Fed up, Daryl stopped talking to them. Lately rumors floated around that Michelina was going to become an animated series. So far, no one approached Daryl about it. He agreed to the interview with Comic Page so he could set the record straight.

"Well, the minute they start asking you 'those' questions, just put them in their place. They're just big babies," Belinda said.

"Shit, that's probably what they think of us."

"Fuck 'em."

* * *

The morning was crappy but productive. Tim Cowan was the engineer for the last two Paw Padds albums. The label thought Pablo wasn't right for them. Belinda knew the game. Tim was big time. She knew him from all the major Cock Rock bands that he worked on as well as some of the mainstream rap artists of the nineties. With those decades of experience, Tim was very arrogant. He gave the girls a hard time on every level of sound, questioning all of their motives. Whenever the band questioned him, Tim claimed that he knew what he was talking about and boasted how he was an essential part in the high sales of the artists he worked with. Belinda told him that she did not doubt his knowledge; she just believed that he did not know the sounds she was going for. The bottom line: Belinda was the credited producer. In the end, Tim acknowledged that and followed her demands.

In the back of her mind, Belinda thought of ways to bring Pablo back.

Daryl showed up at noon. Belinda dropped what she was doing and declared lunch. Jess and Prudee cut out and went to meet their boyfriends. Tim brown-bagged and made notes of their progress.

Belinda saw Daryl's face and knew that the interview bombed. She kissed him and said, "You just left your last interview, huh?"

"Fuckin' circus."

"It was that bad?"

"Well, no. But I feel like shit."

They walked down a few blocks to Le Isla de Encanta and ordered burritos. They sat and ate.

"It started pretty well. She was nice and gracious for seeing me and acted as if it was an honor. Yeah, big fuckin' honor. So we started talking about you, off the record."

"Who brought me up?" Belinda asked.

"I don't know," Daryl honestly said.

"Probably her."

"Nothing bad was said. She just went on about how talented you are and how I'm so great. I started to get bored. Then she said, as if this was going to take my boredom away, that some day when we have kids they are going to be such geniuses."

"Or idiots," Belinda said. "If we're so smart, then it's going to skip a generation."

"It doesn't matter to me," Daryl said.

"Me neither."

They smiled at each other.

"So, she suddenly gets all professional, coincidently when the lattes come. Right off the bat, she asks about Michelina becoming a television show. I tell her that it is all rumor and that I have no idea what is going on. No one gave me an offer and I still own the rights.

"Now that the whole point of the interview is over, I tell her that I'm halfway done with a 4th Michelina book and tinkering with an adult horror novel. I'm pluggin', right? I thought that she might find that interesting. But she stuck with Michelina and starts getting...like a critic. She makes comparisons about me and Michelina - the orphanage and the vet hospital. Michelina's amnesia and mine."

"Oh, that's slick."

"I smelt the goose shit."

"I hope you left then," she said.

"No. Why? Because I'm an idiot. I stayed and told her that all true artists take from their lives and make an art out of it. What's the big deal if I do it?

"She says the big deal is me having no beginning in life. How will I know where I'm going if I don't know where I've been? So I say, what the fuck?"

"You did not. Good for you."

"Fuck, yeah. I was pissed. I told her that my personal life was none of her business and that I know where I came from. Then I left."

"Good."

"I guess."

"What?"

"I don't know. I got this weird feeling way in the back of my head that she might be right. Where did I start from?"

“You started on your own and made something of yourself. By yourself,” Belinda said. “That is who you are and where you came from.”

Belinda looked over Daryl’s shoulder and nodded to him. He turned to see two kids, a boy and a girl, standing with paperback editions of Daryl’s books. They shyly giggled when he looked at them.

Daryl pulled his depression back and smiled at them. “Hey, do you know me?” he asked them.

The boy, the older of the two, showed Daryl the book. “Did you write this?” the boy asked.

“I’m afraid so. You want me to sign them or something?”

The little girl shouted, “Yeah!”

Belinda watched Daryl ask the kids questions and doodle in their books. They were a brother and sister who loved reading Michelina. The sister, Eileen, confessed that she found a white cat and named him Michelina. When Daryl asked the brother, Kyle, what other writers he liked to read, the boy told Daryl that he doesn’t read, but he reads Michelina, he just doesn’t tell anyone. Daryl promised not to tell anyone either.

When Kyle and Eileen went back to their table where their parents waved to them, Belinda took Daryl’s hand.

“That’s what it’s all about,” Belinda said.

“Yeah, I know,” Daryl confessed.

* * *

Life was quiet for the next few weeks. Daryl forgot about the interview and focused on his new book. Belinda finished the album.

Life was normal and secure.

* * *

Until...

* * *

Belinda heard a loud banging from the living room. Sleepy, she sat up and looked around the bedroom. Daryl was gone. Belinda walked up to the bedroom door and peaked out into the hall. From what she could make out, it sounded like there was a struggle in the living room. She heard Daryl call out her name. She went after him.

Chairs were knocked over, the bookcase was flipped down, and the items from the shelves were strewn on the floor. Daryl sat in the corner of the room. He pressed his body to the wall. His eyes looked around the room, blank, like they always did when he was sleepwalking. There was something different in his face. He was scared. Terrified.

Belinda carefully stepped over to him.

"Daryl?"

He remained still, not listening.

"Daryl, it's me," Belinda said, soothing and soft.

Then she saw the blood.

Belinda kneeled down next to him and saw that the blood came from his arm.

Daryl looked at her, recognizing.

"Belinda," he said.

Daryl looked at the wound on his arm. He was speechless.

"Does it hurt?" she asked.

"No, not really."

"Can you get up?"

"Yeah."

Belinda helped Daryl to his feet and moved him to the couch. She gently took his arm and inspected it.

"We're going to the hospital," she said.

"No," he protested.

"Why?" she asked. "Jesus, look at this."

"No. What are we going to tell them?"

"I don't know."

* * *

After waiting in chairs at the emergency room for over two and a half hours, Belinda told the doctor that Daryl was bitten by a dog running around the apartment. She said that Daryl heard it whimpering in the hall and went to investigate. As he reached for the dog, it bit him and ran away.

The doctor looked at Daryl to see if that was how it happened. Daryl nodded, reinforcing the story.

"Are you sure it was a dog?" the doctor asked after he cleaned the wound.

"Why?" Belinda asked.

"Well, I've seen a lot of dog bites," the doctor explained, "but this one is odd. It's almost human."

The doctor looked at Belinda suspiciously.

She gave him the same look back, but with more attitude.

"Okay," she said. "You figured us out. I'm an abusive wife and I bit him. Are you gonna call psyche down here?"

"That is not what I meant," the doctor said. "The width of the bite is wide like a human, but the rip is like... I don't know. It's weird."

They left it at that.

Since they were not sure if the dog had rabies, they stuck around for shots. The sun rose when they left the hospital. Daryl remained quiet until they entered the elevator to their apartment building.

"It was them, I think," Daryl said.

"The Beings?"

"I heard a noise in the living room. I went out there, you know, thinking it was them. I got this feeling. I felt this chill. I just stood there. I wasn't sure what to do. Then something comes at me, like really fast. I didn't get a perfect look, but it wasn't soft and innocent. It was vicious. It tackled me and we struggled around. I can't even remember when it bit me."

The elevator doors dinged and opened.

With the saddest eyes, Daryl looked at Belinda.

"Why are they trying to hurt me? Just all of a sudden. Why now?" he asked.

"I don't know," she said.

Belinda wrapped her arms around him and squeezed hard.

The doors closed on them just when Daryl started to cry.

* * *

The Beings left him alone for a few nights, but Daryl still had trouble falling asleep. Belinda suggested that he use an over-the-counter sleeping pill, but Daryl shot that idea down. He wanted to be able to wake up.

There were a few nights where he fell asleep, but only for a few hours at a time. While he lay awake, Daryl reread his Ellen West novels, finding some comfort in them. Daryl kept as quiet as he could, carefully trying not to wake up Belinda, not knowing she was awake.

Belinda had her own trouble falling asleep. She did not want Daryl to worry about her so she faked slumber in front of him. All night she thought about the new spin on Daryl's problem. Belinda always thought that the Beings Daryl saw in his sleep was in his head and the extension of his sleepwalking. If it was all in his head, then how did he get that weird bite? Belinda felt like she was in a David Cronenberg movie where mind and body were at war. At least, she hoped. That way she knew that it was in his head and not...what? Could the Beings be real? Well, they bit him. Something bit him.

And what about the bite?

A week went by, and it did not bleed or crust up. The bite stayed the same; the skin puckered around the jagged puncture holes.

Like Daryl, Belinda was confused.

* * *

Belinda woke up nauseous.

She jolted out of the bed and dashed to the bathroom. The bile dropped out of her mouth. She continued on, leaving a trail behind her, covering her mouth, hoping to stop the flow. By the time Belinda brought her mouth over the bowl, she was done.

"Shit," she muttered into the toilet.

Belinda sat on the floor and leaned her back against the wall. She called out Daryl's name.

No response.

Where was he, she thought? Was he in the bed?

She called his name again. Still nothing.

Belinda stood up and entered the bedroom, avoiding the bile trail. Daryl was not there.

She walked out into the living room and raised her brows in disbelief. Boards covered up the windows and the front door. Over in the corner, Daryl sat with a hammer in his hand. He slept.

"Daryl?" she asked, moving closer to him.

He opened his eyes and straightened up, panicky. Daryl saw the hammer in his hand and dropped it as if he held something vile. He then looked at Belinda who stood a few cautious feet away from him. His panic turned to concern when he saw her pale face.

"What happened?" he asked.

"Um, I got sick."

Daryl stood and wrapped his arms around her small frame.

"I'm so sorry," he said.

"For what?"

"For not being there."

Belinda stepped out of his hold and motioned to the barricades. "Where did you find all of this wood?" she asked.

Daryl saw the barricade. At first, he looked like he was going to deny it, then he said, "I don't know. I can't remember."

Belinda walked to the boarded windows. "I can't believe I slept through you doing this."

Daryl reached out for her. "You want me to take you to the hospital?" he asked.

"No, but I think I'm gonna go see Dr. Barnes today."

Daryl walked Belinda back to the bed, and then cleaned the puke off the floor. He left the window open and aired out the room. Daryl then made breakfast for them. He fixed toast with jelly and tea. When he walked back into the room with the food, Daryl found Belinda hanging up the phone.

"He's going to see me today at 1 P.M.," she said. "I got lucky, there was a cancellation."

"Great, we'll leave at 12:30."

"No. I'll leave. You have that TV guy coming here this afternoon."

"Fuck. Well, I can call and cancel. Reschedule."

"No. I'll be okay. I feel fine now," she assured him. "You stay here and make a major coup with the TV exec so that you can retire young."

After they ate breakfast, Daryl took the boards off the windows and the door and piled them in the living room. When he finished, Daryl crawled into bed with Belinda, held her, and told her about the Beings attacking him last night. They came through the walls and windows with their hungry and vicious gazes on Daryl. Belinda remained silent, rubbing his head and listening.

Later, they watched television and kept quiet. When it was time to go, Daryl tried to help Belinda change her clothes, but she insisted that she could do it herself. If Daryl wanted to watch her get naked, that was fine with her. They kissed and hugged at the door and said goodbye.

In the lobby, Belinda ran into the super. He looked pissed.

"Hey, Carson. You all right?" Belinda asked.

"Ah, some jerk off went into the basement and stole some wood I had stored down there," Carson complained. "I was going to use it to make new steps for the basement today. Dicks in this world."

Belinda apologized, but did not tell him where his wood was or who took it. She quickly walked out of the building.

* * *

Belinda came home around 3 P.M. Her lateness did not surprise her. She waited an hour for the doctor. Belinda then told Dr. Barnes her symptoms. The doctor performed some tests with her blood and urine; he had a strong suspicion about what could be bothering her. He quickly found the source of her sickness.

Belinda found Daryl sleeping on the couch when she came home. Quietly, Belinda kneeled down on the floor and studied his face. He looked peaceful. Belinda smiled at him and felt proud.

She then noticed the sketchpad on his lap. There was a drawing of a Being, but not the familiar depiction. The sweet featureless wax face of an angel was perverted with evil, vicious and animal. If Daryl was seeing that, Belinda was glad she didn't see them. Then again, Belinda wished she could see them and kill them, leaving Daryl in peace.

Daryl woke up.

"Oh, hey. How did the doctor go?"

"It was good, but I want you to tell me how your meeting went," Belinda said.

Daryl sat up and made room for her on the couch.

"Well, Randy Dulli from Fox seemed like a nice guy, but..."

"But?"

"He was pretty pushy. I felt like I was talking to one of those telemarketers."

"They're all like that. What was the deal like?"

"He offered complete creative control. I can write most of the episodes and even direct a few. He guaranteed thirteen episodes. There's no bullshit with a pilot. Plus, he offered a crap load of money for the television rights of the characters."

"And you said..."

"No."

"Daryl, why?"

He stood up and paced.

"I don't know. It's a big fuckin' pressure. It's T.V. The whole fuckin' world will be watching. There are more people who watch TV than read books," Daryl explained. "I just feel weird about it."

"Well, did you say this to Randy Dulli?"

"No. He just said that the studio is extremely excited about this and they are not about to take no for an answer. He is going to go back to his boss and re-plan an offer for me."

"But you'll probably say no."

Daryl had no answer. He sat down next to her.

"Tell me what the doctor said."

"Oh, not a lot. I'm just pregnant."

Daryl's mouth dropped.

"And if you ask if it's yours, the answer is no," she said triumphantly.

Daryl hugged her.

"This is fuckin' wonderful," Daryl said.

"That it's not yours?"

"Of course."

"Dick," she laughed.

"I know. You want this, right?" Daryl asked.

"Well, I feel like I have no choice, but now that it's here, I'm looking forward to it."

"This is incredible."

"Daryl, please, in the light of this new development, would you seriously consider the T.V. offer? It our line of work, we could be back at Java Joe Joe next year."

"Okay. I'll think about it."

* * *

Belinda found Daryl, again, in the living room. There was no serious re-decorating, but there was something different, writing:

OWEL DANNY SHIELDS

The words were written in pencil, scratched into the wall. Daryl sat against the wall and held a broken pencil.

She woke him up.

"I have no idea what it could mean," Daryl said when Belinda pointed the words out to him.

"The owel part sounds familiar," she offered.

"Duh, it's a bird."

"I know it's a bird." She scrunched her face at him, fooling around. "It sounds familiar another way."

"Oh," Daryl said, smiling at her. "Should I fix the wall?"

"No," Belinda said. "Leave it for a while."

* * *

The pregnancy kept their life happy for a while. In addition, Paw Padds' new album was ready for release. They titled it "Stool Sample." The label decided to give it a push. They stressed the primitive 2 track recording sessions and the back to basics songwriting style to the press. And what better way to re-introduce a band to the press and select public than to have a record release party at a major music chain store. The new album played repeatedly, ingraining it in the guest's heads.

Belinda planned to give her attention to the press for an hour, but when they found out about the pregnancy they kept her longer. She felt bad about it. Belinda saw Daryl standing in the back of the store, waiting for her, bored. She tried to give him some of the attention since he was half responsible for the event, but the press only wanted her. Jess and Prudee, seeing no one wanted to talk to them, snuck out, and kept Daryl company.

When it seemed like the questions were starting to repeat, Belinda stopped the session and walked over to Daryl. She hugged him and said, "I'm so sorry about that."

"Don't worry about me," he said.

"We took very good care of him," Prudee offered.

"Yeah, it was very erotic," Jess stressed in bored monotone. Jess handed Belinda a glass of cranberry juice.

"Mmm. I bet," Belinda said. "Alcoholic beverage, right?"

"Of course," Jess said. "We need more deformed babies in the world."

"Cheers," Belinda drank. She then noticed Daryl looking at a woman standing across the room. "Is that who I think it is," she asked Daryl.

"Yeah," Daryl said. "I've never been this close to her, but I think it could be her."

"Who," asked Prudee and Jess.

"Ellen West," Daryl said.

"Who's she?" Jess asked.

"Oh, Jesus," Belinda whined.

"Who's she?" Daryl asked in outrage. "Ellen West is quite possibly one of the greatest writers of our time. She's the female form of Ray Bradbury or Robert McCammon."

"Who are they?" Prudee asked seriously, then smiling.

"Get the fuck out of here." Daryl waved them off and stuck his tongue out at them.

Prudee and Jess stuck out their tongues back and left.

"You wanna say hi?" Belinda asked.

"What the hell is she doing here? She's been out of the public eye for five years and hasn't published a book in twice as long," Daryl wondered.

"She probably knows someone. C'mon, introduce yourself."

They walked over to Ellen West just as a trendy couple finished talking to the 48-year-old woman.

"Um, hi," Daryl said.

"Hello," Ellen responded sharply.

"My name is Daryl Hersh and this is my wife, Belinda."

"Oh, the focus of all this attention," Ellen said to Belinda.

"Yeah, but if you want it, you can have it," Belinda kidded.

"What do you mean?" Ellen asked. "Do you think just because I don't have the world swooning over me, I must want the attention? Let me tell you something, all of this is a bullshit game. It will kill you in the end."

Ellen downed the rest of her drink and placed it on the table next to her. She said, "Congratulations on the album and have a nice night."

Ellen West left, heading across the room to a crowd of people.

Daryl and Belinda looked at each other, thoroughly confused.

"I swear, I didn't mean it like that," Belinda said.

Daryl placed his arm around her.

"I know. She just misunderstood you or she's going through something right now."

"I'm sorry."

"It's okay," Daryl said. "It's your night, enjoy it."

"Okay."

Belinda moved closer to Daryl.

"My night, huh?"

Her hand secretly reached for his groin.

"Your night," he said, looking around.

"Then maybe we should hurry home."

* * *

Belinda moaned.

"Like that?" Daryl asked.

"Yeah. Don't move."

"Mmm hmmm."

"Get a belly full, sweetie."

Daryl smiled against her wetness.

"Get up," Belinda said.

"You want me to stop?"

"For a bit. I want you to do something for me."

"Okay."

"Grab it. Now squeeze it. Harder."

"Any harder the head is gonna pop off."

"Shut up and do it. You're mine tonight, remember?"

"Of course."

"Stroke it slower. Oh, I like that."

"You're so fuckin' hot laying there."

"Yeah, I know." Belinda smiled. "Now, move faster. C'mon, faster."

"Fuck."

"Mmm. Later. I want you to shoot first."

"Uh, Belinda. FUCK!"

"Look at that."

"Shit."

"Mmm. Keep it up."

"Uh, huh."

"Let's try and break the record tonight."

"How many do you want to have?"

"Eight was the most last time, right?"

"Uh, huh."

"Let's go for ten."

"Damn, you're gonna fuck it numb."

"You know you love it."

"I know I love you."

"I love you, too."

Belinda took Daryl between her legs.

* * *

Daryl screamed in the living room.

Belinda woke up in the bed and ran to him. She found Daryl on the floor with a knife in his hand. Daryl sliced at his leg as if there was a wild animal gripped around it. She saw nothing but blood.

"Daryl!" Belinda screamed.

He continued to slice at himself.

Belinda grabbed Daryl's hand and tried to pull the knife away from his leg. He fought against her, but he did not look at her. It was as if he was struggling with himself.

"Daryl, stop it!" Belinda screamed at him.

He suddenly stopped and dropped the knife. Belinda picked it up and threw it across the room. Daryl looked at her with confusion in his eyes.

"Belinda?" he asked.

She hugged him.

Daryl started to cry.

* * *

Daryl refused to go to the hospital. He feared that the press would become suspicious of why he was back there for another unusual wound. Fine. Belinda sat him down on the closed toilet seat, cleaning and dressing his wound.

"It grabbed me," Daryl whispered to her. He suspiciously looked around the bathroom. "They grabbed me and tried to take me away."

"Where did they want to take you?" she asked.

"I don't know." He looked perplexed.

When the bandaging was done, Belinda kneeled in front of Daryl. She looked him in the eye. They shared the same tired and depressed expression.

"Daryl, I'm scared. There's something going on inside of you. Do you know what it is?"

"No. But..."

"We have to find out. I'm so scared that it's going to kill you. And what about our baby? What if you pass it on..."

"Jesus."

"No. Wait. It's not that I'm scared that you're gonna pass it on. I'm scared that you're not going to be able to help our child when they go through it too. How can we help them when we don't even know what is going on? I love you so much. I need you. I know that you need me. Our baby needs you. Please, let me get us some help."

Daryl looked at his hands. He studied the bite wound. It was still the same, open and unhealed.

"You're right," Daryl said. "I'm just scared. But, okay."

* * *

Dr. Joe Hoffman specialized in sleep disorders. He came highly recommended by Prudee's grandmother who suffered from a bad case of sleepwalking a few years back. Prudee's grandmother was so impressed with the doctor; she continued to stay in his care even after she was cured. She saw the doctor once a month and talked to him about mundane thoughts, often leading to Prudee and how she thought they would be perfect together. Prudee's grandmother feared that if she stopped seeing the doctor she would go back to walking in her sleep.

"Did she sleep with him?" Belinda asked Prudee.

"Eiw, you perv," Prudee shot out. Then she turned serious. "I'm not sure. Come to think of it, she might have."

Daryl dreaded his first appointment with Dr. Hoffman. This was not the first time he sought out a doctor for his condition. He stopped the search six years ago. Daryl felt that the doctors didn't understand him. After two sessions, Daryl mailed them a letter, telling the doctor that he wanted to stop. Daryl did not agree with their diagnosis', which conflicted with what he was experiencing.

"The doctor will see you now," the receptionist said.

Daryl looked at Belinda in the chair next to him. She smiled and wished him luck. Daryl kissed her, took a breath, and entered the office.

Belinda sat for an hour and a half. She read every magazine in the place and played the eye game with the receptionists, finally revealing who she was.

"I knew you looked familiar," the receptionist said. "You're hanging on my son's wall."

"Not naked, I hope."

The receptionists thought about it. "No. I don't think so." She thought about it some more.

Daryl exited the office. He looked mad and frustrated as he walked past Belinda.

"Daryl?" she said.

Belinda chased after him. He entered the elevator and waited for her with his finger on the "Open" button. She entered. Daryl released the button and the door closed.

"Same old shit that I'm tired of hearing," Daryl exhaled. "I'm sorry, Belinda."

"What did he say?"

"The usual: I'm suffering from Sleep Apnea. I told him that that was bullshit because I don't take drugs. So he gives me this look, not realizing that I knew what I was talking about. I stressed that I don't do any kind of drugs, not even aspirin. But, of course, he doesn't believe me. Junkies don't tell the truth. Then I tell him that I have some variable form of Dissociative Fugue. He says that there is no variable of Dissociative Fugue. You can only have one of the disorders. You can't mix and match. Then he goes into Psycho Motor Epilepsy since I have symptoms of night terrors. I tell him that I can see why he would say that, but I have no major stress in my life, nothing dramatic. Then he reminds me that it cannot be Dissociative Fugue because I don't speak in full sentences when I'm having an episode. Like I'm an idiot.

"Fuck 'em. I left."

Belinda placed her arms around him and rubbed his back.

"We can try another doctor."

"I'm sorry Belinda, but this is hopeless. I know myself better than these doctors. Their minds are too closed to help me."

"Then what do you want to do?"

"I don't know."

* * *

Daryl slept in the bedroom. Belinda sat on the couch in the living room and stared at the wall.

OWEL DANNY SHIELDS

Danny Shields could be a name. But Owel? It was so familiar to Belinda but she couldn't put her finger on it.

Another thing that bothered her was Daryl's amnesia. Like his sleep disorder, it was just as strange. Since Daryl was ten years old, he could not remember a single thing before then. Belinda once looked over the police report that Daryl kept just to see if they missed something, but the investigators seemed thorough. No one claimed he was missing, plus there were no previous records of his prints. Like Daryl told her once, it seemed like someone wanted him gone. And perhaps, in some strange way, they altered his mind to block out his past, intending to keep him lost.

But why?

True, Daryl, to her, was the greatest human she had ever met. He was open, sharing, and loving. Daryl never expressed anger to Belinda and he was always there for her, even for the stupid little things. Maybe that was enough. If Daryl remained where he was as a child, then maybe he could have been corrupted.

Tired of straining her brain about it, Belinda kneeled down in front of their video collection and searched for a movie. Among the titles, she found the tape that Kate made. Unknowing to Daryl, Belinda watched it a few years ago. Daryl openly kept it with the other videos, obviously not hiding it from Belinda, so she watched it. Belinda saw Daryl sleepwalk many times before; what she saw on the tape came as no surprise. In a way it was a piece of ancient history. Daryl had a completely new walk now.

Belinda popped it in and watched. It was still the same. Daryl was at his old apartment, playing a game of hide and seek with the Beings that he only saw. In the background, Belinda heard Kate exclaiming her awe. In a way, it was a beautiful sight. A grown man acting so uninhibited, like a child playing a game. It was sweet and innocent.

Getting nothing new from the tape, Belinda stopped it. She took the tape out and placed it with the collection. She sat on the couch and wished that Kate was still alive. They never officially met, but Belinda knew the kind of bond she had with Daryl.

Belinda needed all the help she could get.

* * *

Daryl slept in bed for over a week. They recognized the record made. Belinda was happy for him, and Daryl felt so relieved.

"Maybe it's over," Belinda said.

"No. I don't know. Maybe we shouldn't count our chickens yet," Daryl said. "I don't want to jinx it."

The week went well during the waking hours. Belinda and the girls played a few local gigs and drew in full houses, convincing the label that Paw Padds had a good idea in keeping the tour small and just play the clubs. Plus, now that she was pregnant, Belinda wanted to lower the stress of making big impressions and spending too much money. She hoped that the label would keep the European leg of the tour short not only for her health but so she can keep an eye on Daryl.

Daryl finished the edits on the new Michelina book and sent it to his Editor, Tim Quinlan, at Simone Publishing. Daryl felt confident about the book. He said it could be the best thing he had ever written, at least, until the next one. Belinda agreed.

Randy Dulli called almost everyday to see if Daryl thought about Fox's offer. Daryl let the machine take it most of the time, but when he did talk to Dulli, he kindly told him that he was still thinking about it. Daryl promised that he would get back to him soon.

To celebrate the week, they went out that Saturday. They shopped in baby stores and bought clothes and toys. At first, they were unsure what color to buy the baby since they didn't know the sex. So, they tried to pick out the most androgynous items. They also discussed names. Belinda pushed Jeanine for a girl and William for a boy. Daryl liked the name Jeanine but he favored the name Fred for a boy.

"I don't know," Belinda said. "I hear Fred, and I think of the Flintstones."

"Ah, to hell with you," Daryl joked with her.

"Well, why don't you tell me why you like it," she said.

"I don't know. It just clicks with me."

They left it open for further discussion.

Belinda and Daryl ate out all day and night, and bombarded themselves with shopping bags until they couldn't take it anymore. They arrived home at 7 P.M., falling into bed and into each other.

* * *

There was a gunshot.

No, Belinda realized, it was not a gunshot. Something smashed.

Belinda sat up in bed and turned to the empty spot next to her. Daryl was gone. She left the bedroom and entered the living room. The front door was wide open. The knob and the wood around it had been hacked away.

Someone screamed in the hall.

Daryl screamed.

Belinda stepped into the hallway. Daryl stood down the other end. His paranoid eyes looked around. He held a knife in his hand and stabbed at the air in front of him.

Neighbors stood by their doors, watching fearfully behind Belinda.

Belinda walked up to Daryl.

"Daryl," she said.

Martin Lipton, a middle-aged neighbor in a robe and slippers, reached out for her. "Belinda, what are you doing? He has a knife."

Belinda shook her arm from his grip. "I know what I'm doing," she said.

"I'm gonna call the police," a woman said behind her.

"Drugs," another one said.

Belinda released a breath and shook her head. This is going over the line, Belinda thought.

"Daryl, can you hear me?" Belinda asked.

For a moment, Daryl looked at his wife, but then was quickly distracted. Daryl's arm pulled out against his will. An invisible force squeezed and twisted his arm around, turning Daryl's palm up. Belinda disbelieved what she saw. There was 'something' there grabbing Daryl, but she couldn't see it.

Not able to pull his arm back and just about to buckle to his knees, Daryl slid the knife at the invisible attacker...

...and sliced across his wrist. Blood flooded out as his body dropped from the invisible grip. Daryl fell back.

The neighbors gasped in horror and disbelief.

Belinda ran to his side.

On the floor and on his back, Daryl looked at her, scared.

"Belinda," Daryl said.

She cuddled his head and looked at him, tears running down her face. "It's okay. Don't move."

A neighbor wrapped a towel around Daryl's wrist, absorbing the blood.

"I called an ambulance," someone offered behind Belinda.

"I'm getting sleepy," Daryl whispered.

"Stay awake," Belinda ordered. "You have to stay awake."

"I love you."

Daryl closed his eyes.

"Stop it! Wake up!" Belinda demanded.

Belinda pounded her fists on his chest.
"Daryl!"
Daryl did not wake up.

IV

Bright Yellow Gun
(Inside)

"Daryl? Are you awake?"

He opened his eyes. Daryl had no idea where he was, but from the design of the room, he guessed the hospital. The last thing he remembered was the Beings chasing, grabbing, and attacking him. He sliced one of them.

The room was private and designed with matching bright colors. A nurse in her late twenties stood next to him. She wore a tag with the name Kilfara printed on it. She smiled at him.

"Morning, sleepy head. Well, not completely morning, you still have five hours to go."

Daryl flinched from her over-kill of happiness.

"Oh, now, ain't you cute," Kilfara said. "How are ya feeling?"

"My wrist is sore."

Daryl looked at his arm. His wrist was wrapped in a cast.

"What happened to me?" he asked.

"I better get the doctor. He's gonna want to talk to you."

Kilfara left.

"Wait. Is Belinda here?"

Kilfara did not come back.

Instead, someone new came in.

"Hello. I'm Dr. Ballarat."

The doctor stood over six feet tall and overly good-looking...no...manicured. Daryl thought he looked like a model. He smiled at Daryl and walked over to the chart at the end of the bed.

"How are we feeling," Dr. Ballarat asked.

"We?" Daryl asked. "I'm fine, I guess. My wrist is sore."

Ballarat placed the chart down.

"Yes, slicing the wrist can have a nasty ache afterwards. Well, besides that you are physically fine, but you are not doing well mentally."

Daryl had no memory of slicing his wrist.

"Is Belinda here?"

"No. Visiting hours ended at 8 P.M. It is now...1:13 A.M. But don't worry, I'm sure she'll be here tomorrow. She sat in that chair everyday this week."

Week?

"How long have I been out?" Daryl asked.

Ballarat looked at Daryl, perplexed. "I just told you. A week."

"Was I in a coma?"

"A small one."

Ballarat sat down and crossed his legs. He picked lint off his knee.

"Now," Ballarat said, "you've been in my care for five days. Has nurse Kilfara given you any details?"

"No."

"Good girl." Ballarat looked off and smiled.

To Daryl, it looked like the doctor was thinking of something obscene. About who? The nurse?

"Well, you are in my Clinic. The Ballarat Clinic for Somnambulism. Dr. Ballarat. That's me. We are in Bayonne, New Jersey by the way."

"How did I get here?"

"Well, your case was brought to my attention the day after your so-called suicide attempt. I interviewed your wife and researched your history. It was very interesting, but common in my experience. Your wife thought we could help you, and I agreed. You are not alone here, Daryl. Others here suffer from the same sleep disorder as you.

"Now, it is late. I'm tired. I will stop by to give you a tour of the Clinic and explain more about us. Good night."

Ballarat gave Daryl a big smile and left.

Daryl lay there, a little pissed, but mostly confused.

* * *

Daryl fell asleep. It was deep and free of dreams and violent Beings. He could have lasted until morning, but a scream woke him up. The scream pierced through the walls. For a second, Daryl thought it came from his room.

"No! Get away!" the scream said.

A man, Daryl thought. A scared man. Shit.

The man screamed for an hour, keeping Daryl up and freaking him out. He covered himself with the blankets, curled his body, and faced the door, hoping the screaming man would not come into his room.

The screams gradually stopped, trailing off into crying and whimpering. The Clinic fell into peace.

Daryl continued to look at the door. He waited. He tried to close his eyes but they kept opening up wide. Daryl eventually fell back asleep.

* * *

Nurse Kilfara stood next to Daryl's bed. She smiled and held a tray with a tiny paper cup filled with pills and a cup of water.

"Morning, Mr. Daryl," Kilfara chirped.

Daryl woke up. Her smile irritated him.

"Jesus, would you stop doing that?"

She smiled brighter.

"Stop doing what?" Kilfara asked.

"Nothing."

"Here are your morning meds," she offered him.

"What are these?"

"I just told you. Your morning meds. Meds means medication. Medication means pills, traditionally."

"But what kind of pills are they?"

Kilfara frowned at the pills, confused. She looked up at the ceiling and recited, "Clycxena, Fixerellanon, and Phrasoclyporen." She looked back at him, smiling. "I'm not sure what milligrams they are. I'll have to check your chart. Nurse Cunkphair prepared them."

"Oh, okay."

Daryl took the pills and washed them down with the water.

"Good boy," she beamed. "Now, breakfast is being served in the cafeteria. It is just down the hall on your right, down the staircase to the second floor, and it's right out the door."

"Okay, great."

"There are some clothes issued to you by the Clinic in your closet. Do you need help changing?" Nurse Kilfara asked.

"No, I'll be okay," Daryl said.

"Are you scared I might see your penis?"

Daryl turned red, not even thinking about that aspect. "No. No. I can dress myself."

"Because if you are scared, you should know that I and the other nurses have seen your penis while you were in your little coma. So you shouldn't have to feel embarrassed."

Daryl looked at her, speechless.

"Okay," Kilfara said, satisfied. She patted his thigh and smiled wide. "See ya later."

She left.

Daryl watched the door.

"What the fuck?" he asked.

* * *

Daryl sat in the back of the cafeteria and ate. He picked at a bowl of apricot oatmeal, toast, and orange juice. While on line, he asked the lunch woman on the other side for coffee. She told him, sucking snot back into her nose before it fell into the scrambled eggs, that caffeine was prohibited.

The room was spacious, way too big for the people in it. Each patient had their own table. They all wore the same light gray cotton jumpsuit with Ballarat's smiling face stitched on the breast. Daryl felt like a prisoner. He still disbelieve that Belinda condoned the Clinic. Then he remembered his wrist wound and realized that she was probably scared. He might have died that night.

A few tables across from him, Daryl saw a boy. He was about ten years old with brown hair; dressed in jeans and a transformer T-shirt with Velcro-laced sneakers on his feet. The boy looked scared and paranoid.

Join the club, Daryl thought. Maybe he was visiting someone and got lost.

Daryl walked over to the boy. A patient twice as big as Daryl accidentally bumped into him, knocking some of the patient's breakfast off the tray.

"I'm so sorry," Daryl said.

"No, it was me," the huge patient said.

Daryl turned his attention back to the boy. He was gone.

"You're the coma guy, right?"

Daryl looked at the patient, slightly confused. "What?"

"The guy who they brought in while they were in a coma. That's you?"

"Oh, right. I guess."

"I'm Lixer. How do you do?"

"I'm fine. I'm Daryl."

"Morning, Daryl. I'm gonna eat now. I'll see you around."

Lixer walked off.

Daryl went back to his table and finished his breakfast.

* * *

"Now, mind you, this isn't exactly a hospital," Dr. Ballarat explained in his office to Daryl. "We do a study of your condition. More than anything, I observe you at night while you are sleeping. If you haven't noticed there are two cameras positioned in the top corners of your room. One is a wide shot while the other is a close-up. The close-up is the most important and useful while you are in the middle of one of your episodes. I can study how you react to the Beings that attack you. You looked surprised when I used the word Beings. Well, like I told you last night, there are others here like you and the term in describing them is nothing new. A majority of people with your condition uses that word. And, like you, they went through the same phases as you. Actually there are three phases to your condition. The phase where the Beings come to you in a peaceful manner is Phase 1. They play with you and gain your trust and love. Then there is Phase 2 which is where you are now. They turn violent and evil. Very scary from what I gathered. Then there is Phase 3, a Final Phase. This is where you come to understand why you are being tormented by these Beings and you learn to exorcise them. Your stay here at the Clinic is your opening to Final Phase. The actual exorcism has not been achieved yet. I am still studying the process. It's still experimental, but I am getting close. Very, very close. I hope that you will be here when I discover this cure. I only say that because some patients get very smart and kill themselves.

"We are fully staffed, and we will take good care of you. The nurses will make sure you get your meds, observe you at night, and make sure you don't leave your room at night while in the middle of an episode. Although, your room is locked after 9 P.M., but there have been some patients who manage to get out. Fear can do that to you.

"You will not be bothered by anyone outside the Clinic. We are not supported by any outside organizations or hospitals. We are privately funded by my family. Yes, I came from money, and I am glad to put it to this cause. What you will come to learn during your stay here is that your condition is not rare. Many doctors have yet to acknowledge it. They want to say that it's a form of night terrors or want to pass it on to drug abuse. Then, when they have to deal with the amnesia aspect of it, they just clam up or pass that on to guilt and drugs. Fuckin' idiots. Please, excuse my anger.

"Plus, there are many people from the entertainment industry here. The other doctors have not connected this aspect. Although one told me, it could be the drugs in the industry.

"Again, morons.

"Do you have any questions, Daryl?"

Daryl shrugged his shoulders.

"No," Daryl said.

* * *

"I can't believe you're awake," Belinda said. She hugged him tight while they sat on his bed.

"I'm sorry, Belinda."

"No. Don't. It's over. You're here now and hopefully you'll get better. I heard so many great things about this place."

"You did?" Daryl asked.

"Oh, yeah. Do you think I would just send you anywhere? After Dr. Ballarat talked to me, I checked him out. The man has so many achievements and papers about sleep disorders and amnesia published in these high-class journals. The first time I met him he described your symptoms to a T. I thought that this would be best for you."

"He seems to know what he's talking about," Daryl sighed.

"I think he could be the real thing," Belinda said.

"You look...tired," Daryl observed. "Are you feeling alright?"

"Yeah, it's just...I came straight from the hospital, and I was supposed to go home after the procedure."

Daryl felt the room spin.

"What were you doing in the hospital?" he asked.

Belinda looked away and walked to the window. She stared at the woods.

"Is it the baby?" Daryl asked. "Oh, God. You had a miscarriage. I gave you a miscarriage."

"No. Not that. But it has to do with the baby."

Belinda turned to him with tears in her eyes.

"I had the appointment this morning and the Clinic must have called me right after I left for it. I...I had an abortion."

Daryl's mouth dropped open, but nothing came out.

"I was so scared," Belinda said. "You were in a coma for a week and no one knew when you would come out of it. The doctors gave me the worst-case scenario and told me that you would never wake up. I gave up. I honestly believed that you were never going to come back. Then I thought about having the baby and doing it all over again. Watching them suffer while the Beings destroyed their life. I just couldn't do it. It wouldn't be fair to me or the baby."

Daryl sat on the bed, speechless.

Belinda moved to the chair and picked up her jacket. "I know that this is a lot for you to take in, and that you might be angry with me." She walked to the door. "You need some time. I'll come back tomorrow."

"Yeah," Daryl whispered.

"Please, try to understand. I love you."

Belinda left.

* * *

Daryl was stuck in shock all day.

Belinda had an abortion.

Daryl understood why. It was bad for him to live with this condition. He did not wish it on anyone. He understood that it was scary towards the end. What if he hurt Belinda or the baby? Plus, he was almost dead to the world. He was in a coma for over a week.

A week.

He felt weak.

Fuck, he thought.

* * *

He woke up and saw them around his bed. Soft, wax-like features perverted and twisted into viciousness. Daryl sat up in the bed and pushed his body to the wall. The Beings stood and stared. A smile threatened the corners of their mouths. Daryl felt certain that this was it. They were going to kill him.

The Beings jumped for the bed.

The door opened and three large and greasy orderlies rushed in. They grabbed the Beings and beat them with large black batons. The Beings cried out in fear and pain as the sticks connected with their flesh. They started to fade. A few minutes later, the Beings disappeared and the orderlies pounded empty air.

"I think they're gone now."

Nurse Kilfara smiled at the door.

The orderlies stopped beating and left the room.

Daryl relaxed and sat on the side of the bed. Nurse Kilfara came in and sat next to Daryl.

"Are you all right?" she asked.

"Yeah," Daryl said.

"We saw them on the cameras."

"You can see them?"

"Special cameras that Dr. Ballarat developed. They are not very defined on the monitors. They look like blobs of darkness. The orderlies come in and they start hitting the air, hoping to make contact with them. The cameras are very hi-tech. He's such a smart man," Kilfara gushed.

Daryl noticed how close she was. He also noticed that her hand was under her skirt, rubbing her groin. Kilfara moaned. He quickly moved away and avoided her staring and lazy eyes.

"Thank you. I'm gonna go back to bed now," Daryl said.

"Would you like me to relax you a bit?" she asked.

Daryl hid his body under the sheets, gently pushing her off the bed with his legs.

"No. That's not necessary," he said.

"Oh, it's no trouble at all. It's part of my job. I do it for all the patients and doctors," she explained.

"I'm fine. Thanks."

Her hand coasted over the sheet and rested on his deflated cock.

"You are?" she asked.

Daryl, losing control, started to get hard.

"I'm very tired," he insisted. "I'd like to go to sleep."

Daryl turned over. Nurse Kilfara smiled and said, "Okay. I'll see you in the morning."

She left.

Daryl exhaled in relief.

"Crazy fuckin' place."

* * *

The next morning Daryl avoided nurse Kilfara, but it was difficult. She was everywhere, twenty-four hours a day. How could that be, he wondered. Didn't she go home? In fact, he noticed that all the Clinic Staff seemed to be around a lot, more than the usual eight-hour workday.

Kilfara woke him up at 8 A.M. and gave Daryl his meds. She smiled at him and winked. Daryl ignored her and swallowed his pills.

He then walked down to the cafeteria and noticed Kilfara following him down the hall. She pushed a cart of clean towels, keeping a few paces behind him, smiling. She always smiled at him, and it freaked Daryl out. He felt like she wanted to do more than suck his cock.

She wants to bite it off, he thought.

Daryl noticed that she was watching his ass. He turned self-conscious and started walking backwards, but then realized that she would be watching his groin. He ran for the stairs, escaping her eyes.

In the cafeteria, Daryl took a bowl of cereal and orange juice. He looked around for a place to sit, too many choices to sit alone, too many decisions. He didn't want to eat alone. Daryl spotted Lixir and sat across from him.

"Hey, mind some company?" Daryl asked.

The large man glanced at Daryl and then looked around the cafeteria.

"There are plenty of places to sit," Lixir stated.

"Yeah, but I feel like being with someone for a while."

Lixir shrugged his shoulders.

"Sure. Fine, I guess."

Daryl started to eat.

"Ninety percent of the people with our condition are introverts," Lixer stated with a mouth-full of toast. "That's what Dr. Ballarat tells us. So we like to be alone most of the time."

"I see."

"Yeah, plus, a lot of us are in the entertainment industry."

"Dr. Ballarat had mentioned that as well," Daryl said. He felt like he was talking to a child. Daryl wondered if Lixir was a little mentally disabled.

"What do you do?" Lixir asked.

"I'm a writer. Children's books."

"Wow! Cool! I'm sort of in the same line. I don't write but I entertain children. I do voices for cartoons."

"Oh, shit. You know, your voice does sound familiar."

"You said shit," Lixir said, smiling innocently. "Yeah, I did a lot of work for the Ani-Psycho series and some of those Jap animation movies that get dubbed for the English version."

"Yeah, yeah."

"Now, here I am. They got the best of me."

"The Beings," Daryl verified.

"Yes. They made me shoot my foot off. So here I am."

Daryl looked under the table and noticed the shiny plastic skin sticking out of Lixer's raised pant leg.

"Let me ask you something about this place," Daryl said. "Does anyone ever go home? You know, the people who work here."

"They live here. They have their own rooms in the other wing of the Clinic."

"Oh."

"Yeah, I've never been there, but I heard a lot of stuff from the other patients."

"Like what?" Daryl asked.

Lixir looked around the room and then leaned forward. Daryl met him halfway. "Sex," Lixir said. "But not real sex. You know, the kind you would see in a porno."

"I see," Daryl said.

"I can understand it. They work hard here. They could use the release. Yeah, some of them really like it here. Like Kilfara. She works a lot of over-time."

"I noticed that."

"Did you, you know, put your penis in her yet?"

"No. I'm married."

"So."

"So. I'm not interested."

"Sure you're interested. You just don't want to admit it. What, do you think it's not right to do? It's her job. She's a nurse. I put my penis in her vagina two nights ago. It felt so good. She's really good at her job."

Daryl lost his appetite.

"Please," Daryl said.

"Well, maybe you're still attached to your wife. That is rare for people in our condition. Most of us can't uphold a solid relationship so we have to find sex where we can get it. Nurse Kilfara is so great. She makes me feel so normal, like I'm not even sick at all."

Daryl faked a smile.

"That's great," he said.

* * *

Daryl waited all afternoon in his room for Belinda's visit. The hours went by painfully, but he knew it was worth it. Belinda called earlier and said she would visit that day. Maybe she got sick from the abortion and was resting at home.

The abortion.

Daryl still could not get over it. One minute he felt pissed, the next, he felt sad. But he promised not to take it out on her. Belinda did fear that Daryl was dead to the world.

But still...

Tired of sitting around, Daryl promised that if Belinda did not show up, he would give her a call.

* * *

Group therapy bored him.

Lixir was there. He sat next to Daryl. On his other side was Badge. He was in his late fifties and rail-thin with a shiny baldhead. When Badge introduced himself to Daryl, he declared himself a painter.

Badge came to the Clinic a year ago. He was a part of the first generation of patients. Badge felt proud of that fact since the others of the generations were dead. He explained that it was a sign. Badge was determined to be reunited with the love of his life. Her name was Maria. She hated Badge and his problem. Maria told Badge that he was a psycho and was one day going to kill her. Badge figured that if he could cure himself, he would not be viewed as a psycho, and Maria would fall in love with him again. It was a perfect plan.

Daryl agreed with Badge, humoring him.

Next to Badge sat Glitter, a former assistant director of feature films. She was anything but glittery. She dressed in black and painted her skin black. She told Daryl that she hated her pale skin. For thirty years out of her forty years of life, she painted her skin a dark color so that when the lights went out and she fell asleep, the Beings couldn't find her. It worked most of the time, but not enough. Glitter came to the Clinic five months ago. As safe as it was in the Clinic, Glitter still felt the need to wear the camouflage. Dr. Ballarat gave her shoe polish whenever she needed it.

The most surprising member of the group was Ellen West. She had seemed not to recognize Daryl when she introduced herself to him. Ellen explained how her agent recommended that she admit herself into the Clinic, fearful that she might hurt herself.

Seeing her made Daryl feel...better. He felt less lonely, knowing that someone he respected suffered the same disease as him.

It then came down to Daryl. Like the others, he described in monotone his story on how he arrived. When Daryl finished, he expected a warm welcome, but there was none. Daryl was okay with that.

After group, they went to the cafeteria for dinner. Daryl found Ellen and stood by her table at the back of the room.

"Mind some company?" he asked her.

She stopped eating her soup, placed her spoon down, and looked right up at Daryl.

"Fuck off," Ellen said.

And he did.

* * *

Daryl saw the boy in the recreation room later that night. While other patients played pong, pool, and air hockey, Daryl sat on the couch and paged through a magazine. The boy stood by the door, barely peaking his head into the room. When Daryl moved off the couch and walked over to him, the boy ran away. He stepped out into the hall. The boy was nowhere in sight.

* * *

Nurse Kilfara gave Daryl his night meds.

"Did Belinda call or leave me a message today?" he asked.

Her eyes rolled around her sockets, searching, thinking.

"Who?" she asked.

"Belinda, my wife."

"Oh, yeah."

Kilfara smiled and walked over to the window. She closed the blinds.

Daryl waited for her to answer.

Kilfara walked back to the bed, pulled his body forward, and fluffed his pillows. She dropped him back down on top of them.

"Well?" he asked.

"Well, what?"

"Did she call?"

"No."

"Oh."

"Anything I can do for you?" she asked.

No, you fuckin' sick nympho, Daryl thought.

"I'm fine," he responded.

"Good night."

"Yeah, sure," he muttered.

She left and flipped the lights off.

* * *

Daryl knocked on Dr. Ballarat's office door.

"Enter," Ballarat bellowed from the other side.

Daryl entered the office. Ballarat sat behind a stack of porn magazines piled high on the desk. Ballarat motioned to them and said, "Research."

"Uh, yeah," Daryl said. "May I use your phone?"

"Oh, oh my," Ballarat said. He looked truly worried. "Patients are not allowed to make personal phone calls. No, that's definitely against the policy."

"Well, I wouldn't ask you if it wasn't important," Daryl said. "I haven't talked to my wife in a few days and the last time we talked... You see she just came back from the hospital that day..."

"Oh, nothing serious, I hope."

"I'm not sure. I want to find out."

"Well, since I make the policy in this place: fuck it. It's all yours."

Ballarat picked up the phone and moved it to Daryl's side of the desk.

"Do you need privacy," he asked.

"Well..."

"Yes, I would think that you do. Just press 9 then the area code to call out."

"Thank you," Daryl said. "I won't be long."

"I'll be right outside."

When the doctor left, Daryl dialed home.

A male voice answered, a grunting male voice. "Hello."

"I'm sorry. I think I dialed the wrong number," Daryl said.

"Okay," the man said.

Before they disconnected, Daryl heard a woman in the background moaning in time with the man's grunting.

"Jesus," Daryl said, thoroughly embarrassed.

He dialed again.

"Hello." It was the same man.

"Yeah, I'm sorry to bother you but I'm trying to reach my wife and

I keep getting you..."

"What's her name?" the man asked.

"Um, Belinda, but..."

"Oh, wait. She's right here," the man said.

"Hello." It was Belinda.

"Belinda?"

"Daryl. How are you? Oh, yeah, baby, just like that."

Daryl felt like he was dropping down an abyss. He was speechless.

"Baby, I'm about to cum. Where do you want it?" the man asked in the background.

"On my face, baby," Belinda moaned.

Daryl hung up.

Ballarat came back into the room.

"Everything fine, Daryl?" the doctor asked.

Daryl remained silent. He walked back to his room and cried.

* * *

A week later, Dr. Ballarat entered Daryl's room. He sat down on the chair and watched Daryl on the bed. Daryl was in a daze, staring up at the ceiling. For the past week, Daryl wouldn't eat, and the nurses failed to force him, so Ballarat ordered an I.V. With sad and compassionate eyes, Ballarat looked at Daryl.

"You know, Daryl, sometimes in order to build new, sadly, you must destroy the old," Ballarat said.

Daryl heard him, but remained quiet, contemplating.

Ballarat sat with him in silence for a few hours and then left.

* * *

Group therapy.

"What, you think that you're the first person this ever happened to?" Ellen West said to Daryl. She sat at the edge of her chair, controlling herself from choking him.

"What are you going to do now?" she continued. "Just sink inside your sorry little self. Then go ahead. You know what, if you're taking it like this, then you deserve what happened to you.

"Last year I found my husband who I've been married to for ten years fucking two teen-aged girls in the ass. You want to know why? Because he gave up on me. He was a fucker. He didn't love me. He loved my pussy, but he didn't love me.

"It's the same thing with you; shit, with all of us. People that we loved deserted us. Betrayed. You got off easy."

"How...how did you know what happened?" Daryl asked her. "I didn't tell anyone."

"Fuck! Haven't you heard one word I said? Look at you! You look like us when it happened to us."

Daryl and Ellen kept quiet the rest of the session.

Lixir took the rest of the hour and talked about the rash on his penis.

* * *

Dinnertime at the cafeteria.

Daryl walked over to Ellen's table and sat down. She shot him an angry look while cutting into her pork chops. Daryl didn't care.

"I just wanted to thank you," Daryl said. "You're right. I'm gonna move on."

"Yippee."

"You can be a bitch, you know. I don't get it. You've written some of the greatest books ever. Stories that were so brilliant that they transcended their genre. How in the world could you be such a crusty, black-slimed cunt?"

Ellen looked at him in mid-chew.

The whole cafeteria looked at them.

Ellen laughed.

The other patients turned back to their dinner.

"Fuck! You're just like me when I was your age," Ellen stated. "God, did I hate myself then. Shit, I still do."

Daryl was a loss for words.

"Listen, I like to eat alone. Find me later, alright?"

"Yeah, sure," Daryl said, uncertain.
He left.

* * *

It was late at night when Daryl first heard the metal rattling. He left the bed and looked around the room, expecting the Beings to jump out at him. It was quiet. He had no idea where the noise came from. Then it happened again, and figured out where it originated: the vent.

He looked up at the metal grille. Someone on the other side worked their little fingers through the fins.

"Hello," Daryl said.

"Hello." It was the boy.

"What are you doing in there?"

"Can you open this?"

Daryl went to the desk and brought the chair over. Standing on it, he looked inside the vent. He was able to see the boy's dark form.

"Let me out," the boy whined.

"Okay, okay."

Daryl looked around the room and saw he had nothing to take the screws out with. Then he realized he had fingernails. Using them, he unscrewed the screws in the vent and then took the grille off.

The boy looked at him.

"Hi," he said.

"I've seen you around," Daryl told him.

"I wanted you to see me."

"Well, I did," Daryl said. "What's your name?"

"Freddie."

"I'm Daryl."

"No, you're not."

Daryl flinched and said, "I'm not. Well, then who am I?"

"You'll find out," the boy whispered.

"Okay. Well, what are you doing here, Freddie? Are you a patient?"

"No. I have to show you something."

Freddie turned and crawled deeper into the vent tunnel. Daryl, thinking nothing of it, climbed up and followed.

"Where are we going?" Daryl asked.

"To show you something," Freddie replied.

Oh, okay, Daryl thought.

While Daryl followed Freddie, they passed other grilles. He took quick peaks into them and found the rooms dark and uninhabited.

Freddie stood up on his feet, making his upper body disappear and then his legs. Daryl rushed over to where the boy disappeared. Freddie went up a vertical tunnel with his feet and back pressed to the walls of the vent. Daryl, doing the same, followed the boy.

They moved up through two levels, and then headed down a horizontal path. After a yard or so, Freddie stopped and placed his finger in front of his puckered mouth. Daryl saw a light up ahead, and understood the message the boy communicated. Freddie cautiously moved forward and passed the lit vent.

Daryl followed. When he reached the grille, he peaked inside. Naked people filled the room, tangled together in sex. Daryl recognized them: the Clinic staff. They thrust, moaned, screamed, and panted, freaking Daryl out.

Then someone saw him, looking right at his eyes through the grille. It was nurse Kilfara. She stared at him with an orderly's cock in her mouth. Kilfara pulled it out, drool dropping from her mouth, and said, "Daryl."

Daryl bolted down the tunnel, his heart pumping his brain.

"That was the core," the boy said.

"What?" Daryl panted

"They go there every night to build strength. You caught them on a tame night. Usually there is more blood."

"Someone saw me."

"Then we don't have much time."

They moved on.

Freddie and Daryl reached the end of the metal tunnel. There was an opening, but no grille. Freddie turned to Daryl and said, "Wait here. I have to make sure that it's safe."

Daryl nodded his head and sat down with his legs scrunched up against him. He watched Freddie move out of the vent and enter the room.

This is crazy, Daryl thought. This whole place is crazy.

"Did he recognize you?"

It was a woman's voice. It came from the room.

"No," Freddie answered.

"He's too weak for this. It might be too strong for him," the woman said.

The voice sounded familiar to Daryl. He moved his body to the entrance and peaked into the room. The walls were painted yellow. Freddie faced Daryl; standing in front of a woman dressed in black whose back was to Daryl. To the right of the room was a door and to the left was another door, but this one was green and fuzzy like moss.

"It could be too much for his mind," the woman said. "I think we made a bad decision to do this now."

Yes, Daryl knew the voice.

"Kate," Daryl called out.

The woman turned. She was Kate. She smiled awkwardly at him.

Daryl hopped out and stood in front of her.

"Is that really you," he asked.

Kate just looked at him. Silent.

The normal door burst open. A group of orderlies stormed in. He turned back to Kate and Freddie; they were gone. The green fuzzy door disappeared, too.

The orderlies tackled Daryl to the ground and held him down. They grabbed his arms and legs and sat on his torso. Daryl did not resist.

Nurse Kilfara entered the room. She held an amber-loaded needle. Daryl started to struggle.

"What is that?" he asked.

Nurse Kilfara smiled and kneeled down next to him. An orderly exposed Daryl's right arm and swabbed it with a wet cotton ball. Kilfara injected him. Daryl blacked out.

* * *

Dr. Ballarat sat next to Daryl. He smiled at Daryl on the bed.

"Well, I see that you are up."

Daryl felt weak and groggy.

"What happened?" he asked.

"You seemed to have had an episode, but we caught you in time."

"An episode?"

"Yes. You were sleepwalking," Ballarat explained. "Quite creatively, I'd say. You were in the vents. We finally found you in an empty office, and you were standing on a window ledge. Granted, it might not have been too serious considering you were on the second floor, but still, it was scary."

"I don't remember that."

Dr. Ballarat shrugged. "Hm. Well." He stood up. "I just wanted to make sure you were okay. I'll see you later, Daryl."

The doctor left.

Daryl rubbed his eyes. Last night crept back into his head. Freddie. Kate. A green fuzzy door. Was it all a dream? Kate was dead. A dream would be a logical conclusion, but nothing about the Clinic seemed logical to Daryl.

* * *

Recreation room.

"Sometimes I feel like I'm not crazy enough to be here," Ellen said to Daryl.

They sat on the couch and watched Glitter masturbate with the handle of a ping-pong paddle while Badge tried to stick a string into the hole of his penis. Daryl looked out the window, avoiding the scene. Ellen, on the other hand, watched, fascinated.

"I know what you mean," Daryl said.

"I finished reading your new book," Ellen stated.

"Shit, I didn't even know it was out."

"Yeah, and guess what? As great as I thought it was, it didn't make the Bestseller's list."

"Getting on the Bestseller's list is not my goal."

"Shit, you say that now."

"Yeah, well," Daryl muttered.

"I was on the Bestseller's for five books. Then all of a sudden I dropped. My last three books after that were liners for bird cages."

"They were awesome stories," Daryl said. "You were at the top of your stride."

Ellen smiled.

"Yeah, they have a special place in my heart." Ellen bit her nails. "It's funny how these things happen. I started out working adds for J.C. Penny, trying to pay my rent and publish my first book. After twenty friggin' publishers turned it down, the right one picked it up. It wasn't a hit right away, but it was noticed by the critics. That shit really surprised me, the critic's response I mean. All they do is compare you to great literature like Dickens or Hemingway. God, I hated Dickens, and I dreaded Hemingway. The greatest thing I think Hemingway ever wrote was the blood pattern on the wall when he blew his brains out.

"Anyway, out of nowhere, 'Dove Story' made the Bestseller's. People took to it. I didn't think any one would get it. I mean, it's not like the story was complex, I just didn't think they would get the subtext.

"So, I rode high for five books and then rock bottom. My publisher dropped me after 'Possession' was published. I did find another one, obviously, for 'Going West,' but it was a one-book deal. I did write something after that. It was a period story when America was just being formed, and it involved a witch trial. It was completely unsupernatural."

"I bet it had a magic feeling to it," Daryl said. "It would make you feel magic."

Ellen smiled again and squeezed Daryl's arm. "You're a sweet guy, Daryl."

* * *

Therapy went forward.

During his private sessions, Daryl talked about his life with Belinda and the betrayal he felt during the end. Dr. Ballarat also coaxed Daryl into talking about his parents. Daryl had nothing to offer; he had no memory of them. Ballarat then asked Daryl why he thought his parents abandoned him.

"A part of me thinks that they didn't love me; that they really didn't want me for some reason or another. Probably because of the Beings."

"You are aware that these Beings are the source of your misery," Dr. Ballarat stated.

"I'm not sure I'm ready to admit that."

"Let's see: your parents abandoned you because of them. In fact, every one of your close relationships seemed to be affected by them. They want you to be alone."

"Yeah, that's true."

"How does that make you feel?"

"Angry."

"What does that anger want you to do?"

"Hurt them."

"Hurt them? That's all?"

"Kill them."

"I see," Ballarat said. "That is a positive reaction of your emotions."

* * *

Tim Quinlan was in his late forties and had been an editor at Simone Publishing for twenty years. He signed many great authors and ushered them to the Bestseller's lists, making money for Simone Publishing. He discovered Daryl's first Michelina Show by word of mouth. At the time, Daryl was at a small house and selling well. Tim read the book and recognized it. A colleague of his once told Tim about the book, explaining why he turned it down. Tim thought that that was crazy. He found Daryl and offered him a three-book contract.

Now, in the Clinic's visiting room, Tim Quinlan sat across from Daryl and told him Simone dropped him. Not because of the sales, although, in the company's eyes, that was a good enough reason, but because of the press.

"What press?" Daryl asked.

Tim showed Daryl five newspaper articles he brought with him. They talked about Daryl's mental decline and how children were not safe around him or his books. Parents quoted, "I don't want my children to read his books. You don't know how those psycho people are. They could be putting subliminal messages in their books and make the children perform deviant behavior." A rep from the Catholic Church even said a few words, "Talking cats! Pure witchcraft. Disgusting. It has gone on too long."

"This is insane," Daryl exclaimed.

"No. It's business."

"Fuck!"

"I'm sorry, Daryl."

* * *

Group.

"I have some good news," Dr. Ballarat announced. "I believe I have found the key to the Final Phase. It is still not 100 percent but it came to me in a revelation. I have a good feeling about this.

"So, what I'm asking for is a volunteer. Just so you know, whoever volunteers may not be cured and they might come out of the experience in a worse state of mind. I want to give you a week to think about it before you make your decision.

"That is all. So, who wants to talk first?"

* * *

Daryl woke up in the bed. Freddie stood on the other side of the room. The boy pressed his back to the wall, directly under the camera pointing at Daryl. Daryl opened his mouth to speak, but Freddie placed his finger on his lips.

SSHH. Don't say a word.

Daryl heard the words, but the boy's lips were still. Daryl looked at him, confused.

Just think what you want to say. I can hear you.

What are you, Daryl *thought.*

That doesn't matter right now.

Okay, then, what does?

You, Freddie stated. *You don't belong here.*

Kate told you that.

She asked me to come find you. She is somewhere in the Clinic, hiding.

Is she a ghost?

Don't ask questions like that. It will get you nowhere.

Daryl released a tired sigh.

Okay, he thought. *What do you want from me? Why do I have to leave here?*

I need your help. My mom needs your help.

What's wrong with her?

She can't find me. I need help getting home.

Only, I can't help you.

Kate said you could. She said you would know the way home.

How could I know the way? I have no idea who you are.

The lock on the door disengaged.

Freddie faded away.

Nurse Kilfara entered the room with her big smile. "Everything all right?"

"Yeah, I, uh, had a bad dream."

"We saw you sitting there and staring at the wall. We weren't sure what you were up to. Was it one of the Beings you saw?"

"Yeah. But they're gone now. Thank you."

"Can I help you go back to sleep?" she asked.

"No, thank you. I'm fine."

Kilfara shut the door and walked closer to the bed.

"You saw me in that room," the nurse whispered. "You saw me

with that cock in my mouth."

Daryl nodded, feeling dizzy.

"Would you like to be that orderly? Would you like to fuck my mouth? Make me taste your cum."

"No!"

"Still hung up on your wife. I understand. But remember this, it's all part of your treatment, Daryl. It's all here to help you get better."

Kilfara left. She winked and smiled.

Daryl sat there, relieved. He noticed he was hard. He also noticed that if what Kilfara said was true, that he did see her in that room that night, then Freddie and Kate were just as real.

* * *

"Do you find this place at all weird?" Daryl asked.

He sat in a chair across from Ellen's bed. She shrugged her shoulders, her legs arched up over the sheets.

"Not really."

"This place doesn't..."

"What, Daryl?"

"It just seems so psycho-sexual and tilted."

"Daryl, believe it or not, this place is a mental hospital. They just call it a Clinic so we don't feel crazy. Granted, we don't wear straightjackets or go through electric shock, we see things that the normal world doesn't see. We see Beings that make us feel pain. I'm sorry to tell you Daryl, but you are crazy. So am I for that matter."

"Yeah, okay. Maybe. But I've seen some things. People. People who don't belong here."

Ellen released a sigh.

"Again. My point proven."

"Just listen. I've been seeing this boy. He says that his name is Freddie, and I have to help him get home."

"Why you?" Ellen asked.

"I haven't a clue. But Kate told him that I could help."

"Who's Kate?"

"She was my best friend many years ago."

"This Kate is in the Clinic. She's been visiting you."

"Kate died five years ago. She killed herself."

She sadly shook her head.

"Oh, Daryl," Ellen said.

Two orderlies entered the room. The bigger one pushed a wheelchair. Daryl recognized him from the other night; he had his dick in Kilfara's mouth. Daryl avoided eye contact with him.

"Time to go, Ms. West," the smaller orderly said.

"Where are you going?" Daryl asked her.

"Final Phase wing. I volunteered for the treatment," Ellen said.

"Why didn't you say something?"

"I wanted to surprise people."

Ellen sat in the wheelchair. The orderlies moved her out of the room. Ellen stopped at the threshold and turned to Daryl.

"Daryl. In case I don't see you again, I want you to remember this one thing I'm about to say."

"Okay."

"You, I, and everyone in this place is crazy. Nothing is what it seems."

Ellen blew him a kiss. They wheeled her away.

* * *

The weeks moved on. Daryl kept to himself. At times he hung out with Lixir in the recreation room and played air hockey. Lixir wore a hockey helmet made out of newspaper and oatmeal. He also made noises for the game, simulating the crowd, the action of the puck, and the fighting of the players. It pissed Daryl off but he would rather be with Lixer than Glitter and Badge who were too busy testing the boundaries of their orifices.

No one mentioned Ellen. Dr. Ballarat never brought her up or commented on how Final Phase was going. Daryl wanted to ask, but he also respected Ellen's privacy. After all, it was her journey back to normalcy, and Daryl would want the same if he were going through it.

No one visited Daryl. He received no phone calls. He kept in touch with the outside world by reading newspapers and watching the news on television. Daryl read a few music trades, curiously searching for Paw Padds. He found a couple of reviews of their live shows; all were positive. The critics loved Belinda and the girls. She made a big comeback and the world seemed excited.

He noticed a few articles about himself, a few less than last week. The world was forgetting Daryl and Michelina. Maybe they would remember him when the Clinic released him. That would be far from positive. Local papers would track him down, watching his every move and waiting for him to do something crazy. People would look with paranoid eyes at him. The public might even harass him.

Daryl started to make plans. He figured that Belinda would not take much from him after the divorce. Nevertheless, upon his release, he would be low on money. Belinda always grilled him about this situation. Now he wished he accepted Randy Dulli's offer for the television show. Then again, Dulli would probably break the contract.

Well, he thought, maybe Java Joe Joe would take me back.

* * *

Dr. Ballarat told the group that Ellen felt ready to go through Final Phase. He was so excited; Ballarat invited the group to observe Final Phase.

"Don't worry. Ellen is just as anxious and wants you there to see her victory," Ballarat said.

The group gathered in a small observation room. They sat in soft reclining chairs and faced a wide window. There was a bedroom on the other side of the glass. A large Victorian-style bed was placed against a large window that looked out to an accurately painted city skyline. The colors in the room were soft and comforting; a delicate artist's touch.

Two orderlies escorted Ellen to the bed. She wore cotton, light blue pajamas with little booties attached to them. She made herself comfortable in the bed. Daryl thought she looked twenty years younger.

The orderlies left, and Dr. Ballarat entered. He smiled wide at Ellen, truly proud of her. Ballarat reached inside of his coat pocket and took something out. Daryl couldn't make out what the object was but he saw the doctor place it in a drawer in the night table next to the bed. Ballarat hugged Ellen and said a few comforting words in her ear. He left. The room went dark and fake moonlight shined in through the window.

Ballarat entered the observation room, and sat next to Glitter.

"That's a beautiful shade of green you're wearing today," he said to her.

Glitter touched the green on her face and might have blushed.

"Thank you for getting it for me, doctor," she replied.

"Sorry that they ran out of black. The store assured me that they'll get it back next week."

Glitter and Ballarat smiled warmly at each other.

"Um, so we just wait?" Daryl asked.

"Yes," Ballarat said. "Ellen must fall asleep naturally and go through the motions. She's been up for 24 hours so it shouldn't be too long."

Ballarat was right. Ellen fell asleep in no time.

An hour later, Ellen woke up and stared across the room.

"She sees them," Ballarat narrated.

"Why doesn't she do something?" Lixir asked.

"She will," Ballarat assured him. "This is all part of the Phase."

Ellen gripped the sheets and pushed herself into the headboard. Daryl could see the Beings but he knew that they were close to Ellen.

Shaking in fear, she reached for the dresser drawer and opened it. Ellen took out a revolver. She held it close.

"You're doing good, Ellen," Ballarat whispered. "Make the contact."

Daryl felt confused but he kept his mouth shut. He watched Ellen shiver and jolt. He knew they were grabbing her. Ellen then brought the revolver up, fighting against the Beings gripping her arms. Ellen pointed the barrel at her face and wrapped her lips around it in an obscene fellatio.

Daryl jumped out of his chair.

"Stop her!"

Ballarat stood in front of him and held his hand out, blocking Daryl and keeping his eyes on Ellen. "No," the doctor ordered.

Ellen's body manically shivered. Her index finger pulled the hammer back.

"What are you doing?" Daryl screamed.

He ran to the window and pounded his fists on it, hoping to wake Ellen up.

"It's soundproof, Daryl," Ballarat said.

Daryl helplessly watched Ellen press her thumb on the trigger. He tried to close his eyes to it but he was too late. He saw the back of Ellen's head explode and her body turned limp.

* * *

Lixir, Badge, and Glitter were just as shocked as Daryl. They stared at Dr. Ballarat, confused.

"You'll see," Ballarat said. "In good time."

* * *

A week went by, then two. Ellen, again, was never mentioned. Daryl wanted to ask if plans were made for her funeral, but figured it was taken cared of. If they were, did they all miss the funeral? Meanwhile, Ballarat acted casual, as if Ellen wasn't dead. It pissed Daryl off. How could Ballarat be so insensitive?

The words "You'll See" went through his mind.

You'll see what?

Ellen?

Then there she was. Ellen entered the room while they gathered for group therapy. They crowded around and hugged her, truly happy.

"You're back from the dead," Lixir cried.

"No," Ellen West said. "I was never dead but I am free."

Ellen explained how she survived her head wound. It was just an extension of what she was experienced in her sleep state. Dark matter in her head splattered on the wall, not her brains. The gun was never loaded. It was all part of the therapy. Moreover, it worked. The Beings never came back.

Ellen was cured.

* * *

She was ready to go home.

Daryl read a newspaper in his room when Ellen knocked on his door. Ellen stood with her suitcase in her hand at the threshold.

"May I come in?" she asked.

"Shit, yeah."

Ellen left her luggage at the door and entered. She sat on the bed next to Daryl.

"How do you feel?" Daryl asked.

"Weird. It's going to be weird living a life without them. They were a part of me for so long."

"I think it's wonderful. Was it scary?"

"Yeah."

Daryl looked at his feet.

Ellen nudged him.

"I'm thinking of being next," he said.

"If you're ready to be rid of them," she said. "As terrible as they are, are you ready to live without them?"

"I think so. I need to do this."

Ellen hugged Daryl.

"Then I'll see you soon."

She left his room and the Clinic.

* * *

Daryl knocked on Dr. Ballarat's office door.

"Come in," the doctor said from the other side.

He slipped half of his body into the office. Daryl saw Ballarat sitting behind his desk. Ballarat had a dreamy and tense look on his face.

"Oh, Daryl," Ballarat chimed.

"Um, do you have a moment, doctor?"

"Yes, oh, oh, yes." Ballarat banged on the desk with his fist. "Come on in."

"Are you sure?"

"Yes. I always have time for my patients."

Daryl entered and took a seat. He noticed the back of a head in the doctor's lap. Knowing exactly what was going on, Daryl tried not to look there.

"I really don't mind coming...I mean, stopping by later," Daryl said.

Ballarat slipped down in the chair and placed his arms on the armrest.

"Please, what brings you here," the doctor asked.

Daryl heard squishy sucking sounds.

"Um, I wanted to volunteer for Final Phase," Daryl said. "I would like to be next."

"Really. Well I'm not surprised. I, too, feel that you are...are...ready...FUCK!"

Ballarat's body tensed up, making the head bang the bottom of the desk. He then softly released. The doctor sighed.

Daryl turned red as a crab. He didn't know if he should run or stay.

Ballarat pushed the chair back, making room for the owner of the head to come out from under the desk. It was nurse Kilfara. She smiled at Daryl and wiped the semen from her mouth.

"Yes, Daryl, I think you would be an excellent candidate," Ballarat said.

"Very excellent," Kilfara echoed, leering at Daryl.

'Nough said, Daryl thought.

"Perfect," Daryl said, making a dash for the door.

"Oh, Daryl," Ballarat called after him.

Daryl turned to the doctor.

"Would you care for some?" the doctor asked.

Daryl shook his head and left. When the door closed he heard them chuckling.

* * *

The next day, they moved Daryl to the Final Phase wing. There was nothing special about it. The halls and his new room looked exactly like the other wing. Even the view from the window was the same: woods.

Daryl's medicine changed. The nurses gave him injections instead of pills. They injected an amber liquid into his open bite wound. Daryl asked Kilfara why, and she said, "It's already open to a vein. Waste not wants not."

The injections made him sleepy and lightheaded, but he remained sleepless. Instead, he lay in bed or sat in a chair, dazed. His body felt light. At times Daryl suddenly grabbed onto objects, thinking he was floating away.

He saw a lot of Dr. Ballarat.

"Anger is the key," the doctor explained. "You must pull in the anger and the rage you developed throughout your life. Your parents for abandoning you, Belinda for betraying you, your publisher for being embarrassed of you, your fans for forgetting about you, and the Beings for always being there to torment and frighten you. You must take all of it and channel it through a symbolic instrument."

Ballarat revealed a double-barreled shotgun from under his desk.

"This," Ballarat said. "Yes, it looks like a shotgun. It is a real shotgun but it has no shells."

"Why a shotgun?" Daryl asked. "Ellen had a revolver."

"You are not Ellen. She had rage like you, but hers was not the same magnitude. Daryl, yours is gigantic."

"Great" Daryl muttered.

"So, the key is that you channel it through this. Then you blow your head away."

"Why?"

"Because that is where the Beings hide. Yes, they are in your head.

When they come to you, they escape from your head. It is important that you pull the trigger when they make physical contact with you while they are outside.

"This part is extremely important. It is the key. The piece of the puzzle that was missing. When you make that physical contact, they are a part of you. You can pull the trigger and destroy their nest, themselves, their life source. If you do it when they are not touching you, then you run the risk of them invading your daylight world and they can never disappear."

"It sounds so weird. It sound like suicide," Daryl said.

"In a way it is. You are killing a part of yourself so that you can use that old space to build something new; something pleasant."

Daryl understood.

* * *

With the help of an injection prescribed by Ballarat, Daryl slept deeply. The Beings stayed away; it was perfect.

Except for one night. Freddie tugged at Daryl's eye, waking him up. Daryl tried to focus on the boy but he was very fuzzy.

"The cameras, Freddie," Daryl muttered.

"There are none in this room."

"Mmmm."

"Daryl, we have to go."

"Soon. Tomorrow I do Final Phase, then I can go home."

"You have to help me now."

"I can't."

"I have to get home."

"I promise I'll help you soon," Daryl muttered.

"My mom is in trouble."

"We'll help her."

"I have to get back to her. She's living with evil and sorrow."

"Okay," Daryl said dreamily.

"Daryl, listen to me. She needs me. I'm all she has left. Only I can save her."

"Oh, save her from who?"

"Tarallab."

"Who?"

Freddie faded.

"Tarallab has her and is waiting."

Freddie disappeared.

Daryl stared at the empty spot.

"Tara..." he mumbled.

Daryl fell back asleep.

* * *

They decorated the room exactly like his bedroom back in New York. It amazed Daryl. He could not believe they found all of his personal stuff. Even Belinda's personal items were around. Did she volunteer her collection of ceramic cats, he wondered?

Daryl looked up at the observation window. He saw a mirror, showing his reflection and the room. He figured that the rest of the group was on the other side, watching, impressed with the leap Daryl was about to take.

He sat on the bed and waited for Dr. Ballarat. Daryl wore the same sweatpants and T-shirt he had on the night he cut his wrist in New York. They were perfectly clean and without any trace of blood from that night.

The doctor entered. He smiled at Daryl and held up the shotgun for him to see.

"How are we, Daryl?" Ballarat asked.

"Nervous."

"As expected."

Ballarat placed the shotgun under the bed at an easy reach for Daryl.

"Now, you know what to do. The most important thing is to be brave. You need to be brave enough to want a new life for yourself," Ballarat stressed.

Daryl nodded his head.

Ballarat shook Daryl's hand and wished him luck.

Daryl made himself comfortable on the bed. He slipped his legs under the sheets, nudged his head on the pillow, and took deep relaxing breaths. He closed his eyes and fell asleep.

Deep in sleep, Daryl opened his eyes. Four Beings moved out of the walls. With vile eyes, they watched Daryl. He wanted to jump out of the bed and run away but he forced himself to stay, gathering his courage.

The Beings moved closer.

Daryl reached under the bed and grabbed the shotgun. He pressed the barrel to his forehead. Daryl channeled the rage, the anger, and the betrayal. He felt his hands swollen with emotion, ready to explode.

The Beings grabbed Daryl, digging their nails into his flesh.

Daryl closed his eyes.

He tightened his thumb.

The shotgun jerked up, pointed over his head, and blew a hole into the wall.

The Beings jumped back, releasing Daryl.

Daryl, confused, opened his eyes. Kate stood next to the bed and held the shotgun barrel. She pulled the weapon away from Daryl and tossed it to the floor.

"Oh, Daryl," Kate whispered. She looked so sorry for him.

"What's happening?" Daryl asked her.

Kate grabbed his hand.

"C'mon. We have to go."

Ballarat's voice invaded the room through the intercom. "Daryl, what are you doing?"

Daryl looked at the mirror as Kate dragged him to the door. He saw himself, but not Kate.

"I don't know," he replied.

They left the room.

Kate pulled Daryl out into the hall. A group of orderlies ran towards them. Their features were angular and their eyes were black.

"This way, Daryl," Kate urged him.

They ran down the hall, away from the orderlies. They turned the corner and entered the stairway. Kate and Daryl went up.

"If you're taking me out of here shouldn't we be going down?" Daryl asked.

Kate ignored him, concentrating on her destination.

When Kate and Daryl reached the next level, they entered the hall. They were in the patient's wing. Kate and Daryl passed the nurses station. A nurse stepped out and called after Daryl.

Kate led him into a room. It was Lixir's room. Lixir stopped masturbating and looked at Daryl.

"Daryl, what are you doing here?"

"Lixir, aren't you supposed to be in the observing room?"

The large man shrugged his shoulders.

"We weren't invited there." Lixir released himself and sat on the edge of the bed. "What are you doing?" he asked secretively.

Daryl pointed to Kate taking the grille off the vent in the wall.

"Kate is taking me somewhere," he said.

Lixir looked at the wall where Daryl pointed. He turned back to Daryl.

"I don't see anyone there, Daryl," Lixir said.

Before Daryl could argue, Kate grabbed his hand and dragged him over to the vent.

"In," she said.

Kate led the way into the vent. The path looked familiar to Daryl. They headed for the room with the fuzzy green door.

When they reached the vertical vent that led up, Kate started to climb. Daryl waited for her to move a few feet and then prepared to follow.

The grille that he stood next to dropped off, and a pair of long arms reached for his leg. Daryl fell on his butt and tried to release his leg. The grip was too strong. The arms dragged Daryl out of the vent.

"Kate," he screamed out.

Daryl dropped to the floor in a storage room. The owner of the arms was nurse Kilfara. Her face had the same angular features as the orderlies. Her uniform was ripped in places where her body protruded with unhuman growths. Kilfara smiled at Daryl, revealing gigantic and sharp teeth.

"Where are you going, Daryl?" she asked.

Daryl, on his back, crawled away from her.

"Stay away from me," he warned.

"Baby, I still didn't give you what you want."

Kilfara jumped on Daryl and pressed him to the floor. She held his upper body down with one arm and, with the other, tore his sweat pants, reaching for his penis.

"Let me go," Daryl screamed.

Daryl kicked and squirmed but it was all for no good; Kilfara was stronger.

The nurse grabbed his dick and stroked it, trying to get Daryl hard. He was in no mood.

"Give it to me, Daryl," she warned. "Oh, fuck it."

Kilfara opened her mouth and moved her head down to his limp cock.

A chunk of Kilfara's head exploded, knocking her back.

Daryl stood up and tucked himself away in his pants. He saw Kate leaning out of the vent. She held a bright yellow gun in her hand. It smoked.

Kilfara tried to stand up while she held the space where a part of her head was. Kate fired two more rounds from the gun, both in Kilfara's head. The Nurse went down and stayed down.

"Jesus fuck," Daryl said.

"Let's go, Daryl," Kate said, moving back into the vent.

Kate led Daryl up the tunnel to another level. They crawled a few yards and reached their destination. They entered the room and found Freddie waiting for them by the green door. The boy smiled at Daryl, truly glad to see him.

"Hi, Daryl."

"Hey."

The normal door on the other side of the room started to rattle.

"You have to go now," Kate informed them.

"Kate, I was almost cured," Daryl said.

"That's right. Almost," she responded. "Do this first."

A patch of the normal door blasted out. Daryl saw moving shadows on the other side.

"Where are we going?" Daryl asked Freddie.

"You have to take me home."

"Where's that?"

"I don't know, but together we can follow our instincts."

More patches of wood shot off from the normal door, taking it apart bit by bit.

Daryl turned to Kate.

"Are you real Kate? Just answer me that."

Kate touched his face and smiled.

"I am real in your mind. I'll always be there for you when you get stuck inside your head," Kate said.

The normal door was almost gone. Pieces of wood floated in the air, somehow holding back the shadows trying to break through.

Freddie grabbed Daryl's hand. "Lets go."

Daryl walked to the fuzzy green door.

"You have to open it," Freddie instructed.

Daryl grabbed the knob and turned it. He looked behind him. Kate was gone, and so was the normal door. Distorted shadows floated in. Daryl made out a few familiar faces in the darkness: Ballarat, Kilfara, Glitter.

"Now, Daryl," Freddie screamed.

Daryl opened the green door. Bright green light invaded the room. The distorted shadows screamed in pain. The light felt good on Daryl. He wanted it to never end.

Freddie urged him forward. They walked through the doorway, hand in hand, and left the Clinic inside Daryl's head.

V

True
(Outside)

Belinda felt tired, worn, and scared. Her eyes were red and swollen from crying. She could not believe that her life came down to this.

She sat in a chair in the hospital room. They had just brought Daryl up from the emergency room and admitted him. Machines hooked up to his body monitored his brain and vitals while a few tubes fed Daryl liquid nourishment. His arm was casted where he cut his wrist.

She tried to convince herself that she was lucky. Daryl could have died from the blood loss. Then she saw his lifeless body stuck in a coma, and the lucky feeling dropped. God saved his body but He did not give Daryl his soul back.

A nurse entered the room.

"Mrs. Hersh, there are some people here to see you."

"Thank you."

"I told them that visiting hours aren't for another four hours," the nurse stressed.

Belinda wanted to tell the nurse to fuck off; she couldn't deal with this alone. Instead, Belinda said, "Thank you. I understand."

Out in the hall, Prudee and Jess smiled at her. They held get-well baskets and balloons.

"Hey," they both said, trying to levitate the mood.

Belinda smiled and then laughed. She hugged her friends in a group huddle and released her tears.

"He's going to get out of it," Prudee assured her.

"Yeah, the way he talks about your pussy, he's gotta," Jess stressed.

Belinda laughed through her tears.

"I know," Belinda said. "I know."

* * *

Prudee and Jess took Belinda home latter that afternoon. The plan: Belinda would get some sleep, then go back to see Daryl, but Belinda couldn't sleep. She lay in the bed and thought about Daryl. The image of Daryl cutting his wrist flooded her mind. She knew he unintentionally tried to kill himself. The Beings tricked him. She was positive that there was some *thing* in the hall; some *thing* that they could not see, that grabbed his wrist, twisted the flesh, and made him move. That fact gave her a bit of confidence. If the Beings were real, Belinda could stop them and kill them.

* * *

On the way to talk to the label, Prudee and Jess dropped Belinda off at the hospital. Paw Padds couldn't tour any time soon. The group had to make a few big decisions. Prudee and Jess promised to take care of it.

She exited the elevator and stepped onto Daryl's floor. Belinda passed the nurse's station, waved hello, and then turned the corner.

Belinda saw someone leave Daryl's room. A man. He was fairly tall with long brown hair and a brown beard. His overcoat was filthy, matching the stains on his face and hands.

Belinda flinched and thought, a homeless person in Daryl's room?

The homeless man quickly glanced at Belinda and then moved down the hall in the opposite direction.

"Hey!" Belinda called out.

The homeless man ran. Belinda chased him around the corner, shoving a surprised nurse out of her way, and moving into the stairway. Belinda stopped at the handrail and looked up and down. The homeless man was gone.

The nurse she shoved tapped Belinda on the shoulder. "Excuse me, are you visiting someone here?" she asked.

Belinda turned to her and said, "That guy, you saw him?"

"Yes."

"He was in my husband's room."

"Maybe he was visiting."

"Are you kidding me? Did you see what he looked like," Belinda said. "He was a vagrant."

"I'm sorry. Sometimes they wander up here from the E.R. I'll alert security."

Belinda walked back to Daryl's room. She sniffed the air. It stunk like a homeless person, a mix of piss and B.O. She stepped up to Daryl's body and looked him over. There were no signs of violence on his body, but a puncture from an injection might be tough to spot.

Then she saw it. Moving his bangs from his forehead, Belinda spotted a smudge of dirt. The homeless man touched his head. Belinda hoped that that was all he touched.

* * *

Flowers arrived to the room. Half were from the label and Daryl's fans, and the other half were from family. Daryl's attempt at suicide was in all the papers. Belinda made an effort not to read them, not wanting to upset herself. But Prudee accidentally commented on how inaccurate the information was, testing Belinda's patients.

For the next few days, Belinda separated her time between the hospital and home. She only went home to change her clothes or bathe. Prudee and Jess pushed her to get some sleep, deeper sleep than she would get on a hospital chair. To make them happy Belinda took quick naps. The naps felt deep but short.

Prudee and Jess took turns staying with her at the apartment. Belinda insisted that she didn't need their company. "You're not thinking straight," Jess said. "Just let us help you. Lord knows we wouldn't want to be alone if this happened to us."

Belinda's Mom and Dad called her. She assured them that she was doing fine. Belinda could tell that they were having a rougher time than her. They wanted to come see her but for the last year Belinda's father's cancer weakened him to the bed. Belinda turned the tables and promised that Daryl and her were going to visit them soon.

"Sometime I wonder if you're really my daughter," her mother said to her on the phone. "I really don't know where you get all this strength from."

Neither did Belinda.

* * *

Prudee sat on the couch and watched an afternoon talk show. Belinda entered from the bedroom.

"Sleep any?" Prudee asked.

"I'm not sure," Belinda admitted.

They sat and watched the screen. Normally, they made fun of the guests on the show, but not that day; they had no strength.

"Hey, I've been meaning to ask you, what's with the odd decorating," Prudee asked, pointing to the words scratched on the wall.

"Oh, Daryl wrote that a few weeks ago during one of his walks"

"Why?"

Belinda released a tired breath and shrugged her shoulders. "I don't know."

"Do you think that Danny Shields is from Owel?"

"What?"

"Well, it's obvious that Danny Shields is a name," Prudee said. "I just figured that Owel referred to the town in Monmouth County, New Jersey."

Belinda stepped up to the wall.

"It's a town," she said in wonder.

"Sure, you were there, too. We never stopped there but 9 runs through it. It's right after Freehold."

"Holy shit."

Belinda moved to the bookcase and searched through a pile of spiraled road maps. She pulled out a N.J. map and sat back on the couch. Belinda flipped through the pages. She found Route 9 and traced her finger down until she landed on Owel.

"Prudee, thank you so much."

She shrugged her shoulders, thinking nothing of it. "I'm surprised you didn't catch it," Prudee said.

"I just couldn't remember."

"So you think Danny Shields is Daryl's real name?"

"I don't know."

Belinda picked up the phone and dialed information. She asked for Danny Shield in Owel, N.J. There was no listing.

"Shit," Belinda said.

"Ah, it was a long shot."

"Yeah, but not completely useless."

* * *

Daryl was still the same.

Belinda sat next to him. She inspected his forehead for smudges and sniffed his body for homeless smells. Nothing. Still...she had a strong feeling that the mystery homeless man came back.

Belinda took Daryl's hand.

"How are you doing, sweetie?" she asked. "I'm getting by. It's tough not having you around. I'm hoping that you'll come back soon.

"I think I figured out what you wrote on the wall. Well, Prudee figured out what Owel meant and that was the important part. It's a town on 9 in New Jersey.

"Are you Danny Shields?"

Belinda wiped her wet eyes.

"I've been thinking. I'm gonna go away for a few days. Today is Thursday. I figure I'll be back by Sunday. Some people looked at me as if I was crazy when I told them. 'You're going out of town when your husband just got in a coma?' They probably think I'm going to look for a new husband.

"I'm going to look for you.

"I told Prudee and Jess about it. They're gonna take turns sitting with you during visiting hours. I'm a little scared about leaving you alone. I'm worried about that homeless guy. He really freaked me out.

I also feel a little stupid for being so paranoid. But...this isn't over. I have a feeling that it could get worse before it could get better.

"I rented a car and bought a cell phone. I know. Don't worry, I haven't changed. I just bought one so I can keep in touch. Just in case you wake up.

"I love you, Daryl. Please find your way home."

Belinda kissed his lips, dripping tears on his cheeks.

* * *

The trip took an hour and a half. She drove in the afternoon and coasted fast. Belinda exited the Holland Tunnel, took the Turnpike to the Parkway and, with just a mile on the Parkway, entered Route 9. There was a little resistance on 9 between Manalapan and Freehold, but then it cleared.

Hungry, she stopped at McDonald's and ate. It was around 3 P.M., and pre-teens and teens filled the place. At first, Belinda kept her sunglasses on but then took them off, hoping to avoid attention. She was pretty much left alone. While she ate at the back of the dining area, Belinda noticed a few skaters in their mid-teens spying on her. She ignored them, and they never took it further. Belinda finished her value meal and left.

Motels were not varied in Owel. She went up and down Route 9 a few times before she decided on the Planet Motel. It was in rough shape but it looked better than the one she saw on the North side of town. There were two floors of rooms, and a drained swimming pool next to the parking lot.

She checked in under the name Belinda Kastner and entered the room. It sucked and smelled. Belinda opened the front window and exchanged the bad air for fresh. She stretched out on the bed and took out her cell phone. She called Daryl's room. Jess picked up. She told her the hotel she was staying at and the room number. Belinda then asked if there was any sign of the homeless guy. Jess said that they had not seen him yet.

For the rest of the afternoon, Belinda drove around town, trying to get a feel for the area, looking for some personality trait that was in Daryl that he might have gotten from the town. There was nothing. She memorized her turns and street names, fearing she would get lost. The old and new neighborhoods twisted and turned in the woods.

By 5:15, Belinda started back to the motel. She stopped at Taco Bell for dinner and brought it back to her room. She ate, watched T.V., took a bath, and relaxed in bed until she fell asleep.

* * *

Belinda woke up.

At first, she had no idea where she was and looked around the room. Then she remembered: Planet Motel, Owel, and N.J.

The room was dark; the television penetrated light to the bed. Belinda looked around the bed for the remote. It was lost. Dreading, she left the bed and scanned the floor.

The remote was nowhere. Belinda walked over to the television and turned it off by hand. She turned back to the bed and her eyes glanced at the window.

A man peered at her from the gap in the curtain.

Belinda screamed out and jumped back.

The man moved away.

Belinda dashed to the dresser and searched for a weapon. The best that she found was a metal comb with a pick handle. She walked over to the window and looked out. She saw the parking lot and Route 9. No one was around. She closed the curtains, checked the locks, and went back to the bed.

Belinda recognized the face in the window or at least she thought she did for the seconds that she registered it. It was the homeless man from Daryl's hospital room.

Could he have followed her all the way from New York?

She covered herself with the blankets and faced the door. Belinda gripped the comb in her hand and tried to close her eyes. Falling back asleep was difficult, so she repeatedly reminded herself to find a suitable weapon the next day.

* * *

The records' department was in the basement of the courthouse. The building looked fairly new. It was deep in the woods and separated from the other houses and buildings by a few miles. A large, slightly filled parking lot surrounded the structure.

Down in the basement, Belinda rang the little bell on the counter, signaling the clerk from the back to come out. Belinda expected some little old person, but that was not the case. The clerk looked fresh from high school. New and scabbed pimples covered his face. His hair was spiked and colored green on the tips.

"Holy shit," the clerk exclaimed. "You're not who I think you are?"

"No. I'm sorry. I'm not the woman your father's been having an affair with," Belinda said.

The clerk smiled and waved his hand at her.

"No. I met her. You're Belinda Hersh."

"Guilty."

"Wow." He placed his hands on his hips and just looked at her. "This is so cool. What are you doing here?"

"It's kind of personal so I need you to keep quiet about it."

"Oh, sure. I'm the only one around and I won't say anything," the clerk promised.

"I'm looking for someone. Perhaps a long lost relative. I think he might be from Owel."

"Okay. Give me the name, and I'll go see what we have."

"Danny Shields or Daniel."

The clerk nodded his head, perhaps committing it to memory, and went to the back.

Belinda roamed around the room. There was not much to do but stare out the window high on the wall. It looked out to the parking lot. She watched a prowl car park, and a police officer usher a man in cuffs to the building.

The clerk returned. He held a folder and opened it up on the counter.

"Well, it seems like we have all the vitals for Daniel Shields. Birth, marriage and death," he pointed out to her.

Belinda looked at them and frowned at the death certificate.

"Daniel died in 1985. He was shot," she observed. She looked at the birth certificate and checked out the birth date. "That would have made him thirty one when he died."

"Is he your man?" the clerk asked.

"No. But I'm not sure."

Belinda studied the marriage certificate. Daniel and Tanya Deal married when they were eighteen. Belinda guessed they were high school sweethearts.

"You know, this name sounds familiar," the clerk said.

"How so?"

"I think he was part of a murder or something. I'm not sure. I was just three when it happened. You might want to ask Shelly Sully. She works over at the periodicals in the library. Shelly has been doing it for years. Plus, I hear she has a photographic memory. If she read a sales ad for Jamesmart a billion years ago, she could tell you what issue she read it in. Freaky."

"A billion years ago, huh," Belinda kidded. "She must be pretty old."

"Ancient."

"Cool. Thanks. Can you check something else? Can you see if there is a death certificate for Tanya Hersh or Deal and maybe see if there are any birth certificates after them under the Shields name."

"You wanna see if they had a child. Okay, what year do you think they were born?"

"Mid to late seventies."

"That will take a bit. We're like the last department to go to computer files, so I'll have to do some searching."

Belinda smiled sweetly at him and said, "Thanks, I really appreciate this."

The clerk blushed and disappeared to the back. Moments later, he returned empty handed.

"So that means that she's alive, and they had no children?" she asked.

"Not necessarily," the clerk responded. "It could mean that she didn't die in this town. If Tanya moved, say to Freehold and died, they might have her certificate there. Same thing with their child. There is no record of a birth or death, but that might not be true in other towns."

"Well, this is still great," Belinda said.

"It helps?"

"Yes. Thank you so much. Can I get copies of these and the address for the library?"

"The copies will cost ya cash, but the address will cost ya an autographed CD. I have one in my bag," he said cautiously.

Belinda smiled.

"Deal," she said.

* * *

The library was ten minutes away. Like the courthouse, the building looked new, surrounded by concrete and trees. Unlike the courthouse, there was a police station next door.

Belinda walked up to the counter of the periodicals department and smiled at the librarian. The name on her tag said Sully. She was in her early eighties, scrawny, and looked mean as hell. She glared with condescending eyes at Belinda.

"Yes. How may I help you," Sully said dryly.

"You are Shelly Sully?"

"Yes. Who are you?"

"I'm Belinda Hersh. I was told by the clerk at the records' department that you could help me."

"Kevin," she drawled with disgust. Sully looked Belinda over. "Yeah, you look like you would know Kevin."

Belinda frowned.

"Yeah, well, he said you could help me with some local information."

"What do you want to know?"

"I'm looking for a Daniel Shields-"

"Well, you are not going to find him," Sully interrupted.

"Yes, I know. But Kevin said that there might be a story about that. Stuff from the papers."

"Oh, Jesus. What is with your kind?"

Belinda flinched and said, "Excuse me."

"You freaks," Sully spit out. "You are so hungry for morbid information. Why is your kind so obsessed with death?"

"I assure you, I am not looking for masturbation material."

Sully's eyes widened.

"I'm here on family business," Belinda said. "I believe Daniel Shields might be related to my husband in some way."

"Who's your husband?"

"Daryl Hersh."

"The writer. I read that he's in a coma in New York."

"He is."

"Drugs?"

"Fuck you," Belinda spat out. "This is useless. If you're not going to help me, I wish you would say it instead of having me stand here and take your abuse."

Sully cold-stared at Belinda, and then tore a smile across her face. Sully exploded into laughter.

"Oh, boy. Okay," Sully said. "You wait right here."

Belinda had no idea what just happened, but she was glad it turned around to the positive. She leaned against the counter and rubbed her head, dulling the aggravation she just went through.

Shelly Sully came back with a few microfilm cassettes and walked Belinda to the machine across the room. They sat next to each other. Sully threaded the cassette and navigated it with the shuttle wheel of the machine.

"Danny Shields. Never met him. Had no reason to," Sully said. "Before he died he was an average guy. Here it is."

Belinda looked at the article. Tanya found Daniel Shields murdered in his bedroom. Someone broke into the house and shot him in the head. The unidentified assailant then kidnapped their ten-year-old son Fredrick Shields. Tanya didn't see who did it, but she blamed a Doctor

Tarallab who Daniel claimed was seeing during his last days. The police never found any Doctor Tarallab anywhere in the United Stated.

"He did have a son," Belinda whispered to herself.

"Yep. The boy. They never did find him. My brother-in-law was a detective on the case back then. He said that they didn't have a lot to go on. The kid was taken without a trace."

"That's it?"

"There are a few more articles that reveal nothing new. Like I said, the kid nor the murderer was ever found. They looked at everyone in their lives. The reporters even made some broad leaps, stating that Daniel was murdered by his wife and his brother, saying that they were having some kind of affair. When you think about it, it could be possible. Ray Shields mysteriously disappeared that night as well."

"Is Tanya Shields still alive?"

"Beats me."

"Can I get copies of these?" Belinda asked.

"Yep," Sully sighed.

Sully found the articles and printed them out on a photocopier next to the machine. Sully picked up the copies and gave them to Belinda.

"I was just thinking," Belinda said. "Could I speak to your brother-in-law about this?"

"Sorry. He died three years ago."

"Oh."

"Anything else you need?"

"I guess not. Thanks a lot for your help."

Sully gathered the cassettes and turned the machine off. "I hope your husband gets better," she said and then left.

* * *

Belinda sat in her car in the library parking lot. She looked over the articles and studied the pictures of the Shields family. One picture of the family looked like it was taken at some department store. Danny and Tanya Shields posed behind Fred Shields who sat on a stool. They smiled wide, truly happy, Belinda believed. Freddie Shields, although age ten in the picture, looked a little like Daryl. She remembered the picture of Daryl that the police took of him when he was found. Daryl had short blond hair and wore dirty clothes as if he was on the streets for months. It was possible that they could be the same.

There was also a picture of Ray Shields. The picture was natural and taken in a house: probably from some family function. Ray looked normal, nondescript, but Belinda saw something in his face that she recognized. She chalked it up to family resemblance from the other pictures. But there was something else weird about his face. Something dark, like Ray knew something that no one else did. Could he have killed Danny Shields, she asked herself.

Where to next?

Belinda searched for the Shields' house using the address from the news articles. She found it in an older development. She parked the car in front of the house on Tunisia Ave. Belinda stepped out and stood on the decrepit sidewalk. She stared at house 256. It was more run down than the others. An Otto Realtor For Sale sign stuck out of the patched and wild lawn. The windows were boarded up, and the shrubs that lined the edge of the house were dead and bald. The place gave Belinda a cold chill.

She walked up to the front door. She tried the knob and found it open. Belinda peaked inside the house. It was dark, and decay wafted out.

"You don't want to go in there."

Belinda turned to a little girl standing on the lawn next door. She was seven or eight years old and wore jeans, a ducky T-shirt, and an opened winter jacket with a backpack stuffed to the seams at her feet.

Belinda smiled at the little girl and asked, "Why not?"

"There are ghosts and monsters in there," the little girl said.

"You live over here?" Belinda asked, pointing to the house next door.

"Yeah."

"What's your name?"

"Betty."

"Hi, Betty. I'm Belinda. Is your mommy home?"

"Yeah. She should be. She's always home when I get out of school."

"Can I talk to her? Can you get her for me, sweetie?"

Betty looked up at the sky and then said, "Yeah." She ran with her book bag into the house.

Belinda smiled at her. She hoped that if she had a little girl she would be as cute as Betty.

The mother came out of the house. She was about Belinda's age, maybe younger. The mother looked a lot like the daughter, but older and worn. She hugged her sweater around her body and walked closer to Belinda.

"Hi. I'm Belinda Hersh." She held her hand out to the mother. They shook.

"Hi. I'm Susan. Betty said you wanted to talk to me," the mother said.

Belinda saw Betty waiting at the front steps of the house, twisting her body around the pole of the awning, watching.

"Yeah, I had some questions about this house. I was wondering if you could help me out," Belinda asked.

"You gonna buy it?"

"Um, maybe."

"They got real-estate agents for that."

"Yes. Yes, they do. But I don't trust them too much. I know they're supposed to disclose all information on the house, but I've seen Amityville Horror too many times."

Susan smiled.

"Yeah, I'm sure they would soften up the house for ya."

"How long have you lived next door, Susan?"

"Going on seven years."

"It's always been like this?"

"Yeah. I don't think anyone lived here since the murder. Too many stories make it unattractive."

"Ghosts and stuff," Belinda offered.

"And monsters!" Betty screamed from the front steps.

Belinda looked at Susan to see if it was true. Susan shrugged.

"I've never seen anything and I stress seen," Susan said.

"Well, what did you hear?" Belinda tested.

"I don't know. I hear, and this is just what my imagination interprets, a grunting sound. It comes from inside like there's some wild animal in there...searching."

"You heard this at night?"

"Yeah. But not in a few weeks, though. I used to hear it every week."

"I saw the monster!" Betty announced.

"Would you mind?" Belinda asked Susan, motioning to Betty.

"Sure, I guess not."

Belinda stepped over to Betty. The little girl met Belinda halfway on the lawn.

"What did you see?" Belinda asked.

"I saw a monster going and leaving the house. He passes my window," Betty whispered.

"When he's coming and going do you see or hear a car?"

Betty scrunched her face at Belinda.

"No," Betty said. "Monsters don't drive cars."

"No, I suppose they don't."

"That would be silly."

"Did you see what it looked like?"

"No."

"You still think you're gonna buy the house?" Susan asked.

Belinda turned to Susan and shrugged her shoulders. "I don't know."

"Well, my husband says that those noises I've been hearing could be from the foundation. This development is old. One of the oldest for the town and they weren't made too well. The basements are bigger than the houses. Don't make sense, right? So, they could crumble in. My husband reinforced ours. He's a contractor. In fact, he worked on a lot of houses in this neighborhood. If you buy the house, I'm sure he'll make you and your husband a good deal."

"So, you don't think there are any monsters in there?" Belinda asked.

The mother blurted out a laugh and covered it with her hand.

"No. There's no such thing as monsters, but it is kinda fun to be scared about it, like living in a horror movie or something."

Belinda smiled and said, "Yeah, I know what you mean. Hey, do you know Tanya Shields or Tanya Deal?"

Susan shook her head.

"No, but isn't Shields the previous owner?" Susan asked.

"Yeah, I wanted to ask her about the house, too."

"Sorry. Can't help ya."

Susan hugged her body, shivering off a chill.

"We should be getting inside," the mother said.

Belinda thanked them for their time and watched the mother and daughter enter the house. Belinda walked to her car and sat in it, warming up the engine. She watched the house, and thought about what Betty and Susan said: unconfirmed monsters coming and going in the house, searching. What were they searching for? Daryl? Freddie?

* * *

It was getting dark, and Belinda was hungry. She spotted the Silver Bell Diner on Rte 9 and decided to buy dinner there. First, she wanted to stop at Jamesmart.

In the sporting goods department, Belinda checked out the hunting knives in the glass display case. She considered getting a gun but decided that it would be too complicated. Belinda bought a five-inch hunting knife with a serrated blade on one side and a saw edge on the other. The sales boy looked at Belinda as she practiced stabbing the air. He must have thought that Belinda was a psycho, but she did not care.

* * *

The Silver Bell Diner was busy. Belinda took a seat at the front counter. She sat between two elderly people, a man and a woman, who looked at her suspiciously and moved their belongings away. Belinda smiled it off and studied her menu. She gave the waitress her order and waited for her food. To pass the time, Belinda looked over the news articles from the library and the vital certificates.

The older woman at Belinda's right gathered her belongings and left. Belinda took advantage of the space and looked around the diner. She checked out the patrons and the staff. Belinda was anxious. She hated sitting and doing nothing.

Belinda checked her watch; it was just after seven. Visiting hours at the hospital would end at eight. Belinda took out her cell phone and dialed Daryl's room. The call did not go through.

Belinda waved over her waitress and told her that she had to step out a second to make a phone call. The waitress looked at her suspiciously, released a sigh, and said okay.

Outside on the steps, Belinda dialed the hospital. Prudee picked up.

"How's he doing?"

"Bel, oh, he's fine. The same," Prudee said. "How are things in bumble-fuck?"

"Eh, pretty good."

"Was Daryl from there?"

"I'm not 100 percent positive, but I think I'm almost there."

"Cool. Wish I could tell you something new. Something good."

"I know. So do I."

A waitress in her late forties came down the steps and stopped near Belinda. Belinda and the waitress shared a smile. The waitress lit a cigarette and looked out at the traffic on 9.

"Listen," Belinda said, "you haven't seen that guy, have you?"

"That homeless person? No."

"I didn't think so."

"That's good, right?"

"For Daryl," Belinda said.

The bored waitress turned to Belinda. She noticed the waitress's name tag: Tanya.

"Helloooo," Prudee called.

"Um. Yeah, sorry. I have to go. My food is here."

They said good-bye. Belinda slipped the phone in her jacket.

Tanya, the waitress, nodded towards the diner doors. She said, "You have an order waiting in there."

"Yeah, I just had to make a call."

"Sheryl wasn't sure if you were legit," Tanya said. "Wanted me to keep an eye on you during my break. Don't take it personal."

"I won't. It's cool."

"Yeah. We get a lot of jerks that step out on their bills. Boss makes us pay for them," Tanya sighed. "Every little bit helps."

Belinda offered her hand.

"I'm Belinda Hersh."

The waitress shook it and pointed to her name tag. "Tanya, as you probably saw."

Belinda smiled at her.

"Yeah, I did."

"You're new in town," Tanya stated.

"Just passing through," Belinda said. "How can you tell?"

"Lucky guess in a way. I've worked here for almost ten years. I see a lot of local faces. You don't look familiar."

"Shit, waitressing for ten years. You must have nerves of steel."

Tanya shrugged her shoulders and said, "Ass of steel, too. Beats being homeless, though."

"I hear ya."

"What about you? Let me guess. You're a musician. That or you work in a music store."

"Musician."

"Have I heard of you?"

"I'm in a group called Paw Padds."

Tanya shrugged.

"Sorry, but I don't listen to the radio."

Tanya took out another cigarette. She offered one to Belinda.

"Oh, no thanks. I'm pregnant," Belinda said.

Tanya lit up.

"Congratulations," she said, nodding her head.

"Yeah, it's pretty weird," Belinda said. "Certainly changes your perspective and opens your life up, you know."

"They sure do."

"You have any kids?" Belinda asked.

Tanya focused on her cigarette.

"No," she said, dropping the cigarette on the floor and stomping it out with her foot. "My break is up. It was nice meeting you."

Tanya smiled and walked back in.

Belinda followed and then sat on her stool at the counter. The food was waiting for her. Belinda ate and kept an eye on Tanya while looking at the photocopy of the Shields family.

* * *

After eating her dinner, Belinda bought a large coffee and sat in her car in the parking lot of the Silver Bell Diner. She waited and watched for Tanya to leave.

The waitress didn't leave until midnight. Belinda almost missed Tanya due to her dozing. She watched Tanya walk to her mid-70s car coated with primer. The car took some coaxing but it started up.

Belinda followed Tanya down 9 South. She turned off a side road just before the border of Lakewood. Once they passed a few closed strip malls, the dark woods engulfed them. After a few more turns, Tanya entered a housing development. The waitress parked her car on the driveway of a one story house and walked up to the front door.

Belinda parked the car one house away across the street. She watched Tanya enter the house. A light went on in the front. It flickered and changed color. Belinda figured it was the television.

Belinda took out her cell phone and dialed information. She gave the address of the house and asked for the number of Tanya Deal or Shields. The operator told Belinda that there was no Tanya Shields listed but there was a Tanya Deal. Unfortunately, the number was unlisted. Belinda thanked her and hung up.

I got ya, she thought triumphantly.

Belinda watched the house for another hour before she started falling asleep. She snored loudly.

* * *

"Hey!"

Belinda woke up in the car and found Tanya banging her morning paper on the windshield. The waitress wore sweats, a T-shirt, and a pissed off expression.

"Hey. What are you doing?" Tanya asked.

Belinda turned red with embarrassment. She rolled the window down.

"What? Excuse me."

"Don't give me that innocent crap," Tanya warned. "I saw you out here last night. Now, here you are this morning. I go to see who the hell you could be, and I recognize you from the diner last night. Looks to me that you're following me."

"No. No. I...Oh, shit."

"Yeah, oh shit is right," Tanya said. "Now you listen closely. I got enough worries in my life that I need some obsessive lesbo harassing me. I don't eat pussy. Never had and never will. Now you have to go home and make the effort in never running into me again."

Tanya turned back to her house.

Belinda stepped out of the car and walked after her.

"Wait. You have the wrong idea."

Tanya kept walking, holding her hand out in Belinda's direction and deflecting her words. "I don't want to hear it." Tanya stopped at her door.

Belinda threw her arms in the air, stomping her feet on the asphalt in frustration.

"Fredrick Shields," Belinda called out.

Tanya froze with her hand on the door, dropping the newspaper to the ground. She turned with the most horrified expression on her face to Belinda. The waitress rushed over to Belinda, looking around for spying ears and eyes. They were alone.

"Don't you ever say that name here," Tanya warned. "You have no right to say that name."

"I'm afraid I do. He's your son, right?"

"Just shut up."

"Well, if he is, that would make you my mother-in-law because Fredrick Shields is Daryl Hersh," Belinda pressed.

"You are insane. Get the fuck away from me," Tanya said, walking back to her house.

Belinda chased after her and said, "Wait."

"Go away, please."

"You don't understand."

Tanya turned to Belinda at the open front door and lowered her voice. "No. You don't understand." Tanya closed the door.

"Please, open up. They are the same. Daryl, my husband, was found on a train. He was ten years old; the same age as Fredrick when he was kidnapped. You have to help me. I don't know what else to do for him. Please."

No answer.

Belinda released a breath.

"Okay. I understand that this might be too much. I'm gonna write my number here on your newspaper. When you're ready to talk, please call me."

Belinda placed the paper by the door.

"Please call," Belinda whispered.

* * *

Belinda entered her motel room, locked the door, and fell into bed. She felt tired, worn, and helpless. Belinda cried, then went to sleep.

* * *

A chirping woke her up. It was the cell phone. Belinda sat up quickly in the bed, making her head spin. She went over to her jacket on the floor and took the phone out.

"Prudee?" Belinda asked.

"No."

A woman's voice. Belinda heard people and banging dishes in the background.

"Tanya?"

"Come to the diner tonight. I get off at 7 P.M.," Tanya said.

"Okay. Thank you."

"Yeah. Whatever."

Tanya hung up.

Belinda sat on the edge of the bed. She had no idea how to take the request.

* * *

Tanya waited in a booth at the back of the diner and drank a cup of coffee. Belinda smiled at her, but Tanya was too tired to return it. Belinda sat across from her.

"You want some coffee?" Tanya asked.

"Um, sure. That would be great."

Tanya walked over to a station against the wall and made a cup. She placed it in front of Belinda.

"Thanks," Belinda said.

"De nada."

"So, I'm curious. Why are you talking to me now?" Belinda asked.

"We can't talk at my house."

"Why?"

"My, uh, husband was home."

"He doesn't know about your past?"

"Oh, he knows all right. I just don't bring it up. He gets upset whenever I mention it, you could say."

"Does he hit you?"

"Listen, are we going to talk about Freddie or what?" Tanya asked.

"Yes." Belinda sighed. "Sorry."

"Tell me about your husband...what's his name? Daryl?"

"He's...shit, he's wonderful. I love him. There's no one in the world like him."

"What does he do?"

"He's a writer. Children's books. You know the series The Michelina Show?"

Tanya shook her head sadly and then smiled.

"What?" Belinda asked.

"Does he know where he got the name Michelina from?"

"No. He said he just likes it."

"That's odd."

"Not really. If it were from his past, he wouldn't remember. Daryl has amnesia."

"Jesus. Still?"

"Where is Michelina from?"

"Freddie's Uncle Ray had a cat named Michelina. A shorthaired European. All white-"

"With a patch of gray hair on the top of its head," Belinda finished. "Yep, that's the cat he writes about."

"He's not here with you, is he?"

"No. He's in New York. He's in a coma."

"What happened?" Tanya asked.

Belinda told her all the events that led to the coma. Tanya looked less than surprised. She nodded her head in understanding.

"He was suppose to die," Tanya stated. "Shit, this was not how it was supposed to go."

"That story I read in the paper, what you told the police, it was fake, right?"

Tanya nodded.

"Sort of. We couldn't tell the whole truth," Tanya said.

"And that was?"

Tanya moved her head across the table. Belinda met her halfway.

"The Beings have been in Danny's family for...shit, forever, probably. They drove his father to kill himself and his father before him.

"Danny was so happy that night. I didn't expect anything like that to happen."

* * *

"The day went so well. For the first time in months we, as a family, were happy...connected, you know. Things had been so weird and strange. Danny was paranoid, scared. He blocked me out. He wanted to get better, but he didn't want my help. Danny thought that I wouldn't understand, wouldn't be able to help. He was probably right. I still don't understand it all.

"So he started seeing a doctor. I found his card one day. I went to check this guy out and visited the address on the business card. There was no doctor's office there. It was completely abandoned. But I did see Danny enter the building, so I followed him in. The place was disgusting. It had this dead smell. There was no furniture, no paint on the walls, nothing. Danny wasn't even around, but something else was. I felt a chill. I heard this wheezing like a... I don't know. I left. I was too freaked out to stay.

"Obviously this guy wasn't a real doctor. Instead of getting better, Danny got worse. He disappeared for hours, then days. He quit his job just to see this Dr. Tarallab.

"Anyway, Danny shot himself in the head in our bedroom. I was in the living room, sleeping, when it happened. God. I went in there...and...Danny was on the bed...with his eyes opened and his...the back of his head on the wall.

"I, uh, heard a whimpering. I found Freddie in the closet. The door was wide open, and his body was nudged against the wall. He just stared at his father. Freddie's jaw moved around like he wanted to say something. I tried to get him to stop looking at his father but he would just look around me or start to shake in a panic. I didn't want to make it worse, so I just left him in the closet.

"I called Ray. I should have called the police first, but I didn't think they would understand. As much as it looked that Danny shot himself, I still couldn't accept that he did it. I had this strong feeling, you know, in this instinct kind of way, that he was murdered. When Ray came over I told him everything. He didn't look too surprised. Ray was expecting this to happen. But he always thought that he would be the first one to go. Ray saw the Beings also.

"Anyway, Ray went into the bedroom, said good-bye to Danny, and closed his eyes. He then went to the closet and tried to get Freddie out.

"'Hey, Fred,' he said. Just like that, as if nothing was going on.

"Freddie looked right past him and said, 'Who?'

"'Fred. Isn't that your name, kid?' Ray asked.

"'I don't know,' Freddie said to him.

"Ray turned to me as if I knew what was going on. I hadn't a fuckin' clue so he turned back to Freddie.

"'Do you know who I am?' Ray asked him.

"Freddie looked at Ray, really looked at him as if he really wanted to recognize him. Freddie just gave up and shook his head no.

"'Do you know who she is?' Ray asked him.

"Freddie looked at me and made the same face. I couldn't help it, I started crying. That confused Freddie even more. He said Freddie had amnesia. Ray thought that that was great. I asked him how could this be great.

"'This gives him a fighting chance,' Ray said. 'He's not seeing the Beings yet, right? Well, if he could start up a new life where they couldn't find him, he just might make it past forty. He won't remember where he came from. We just have to hope that he never remembers. Shit, I would think watching his father blow his brains out would do it.'

"I told him that that was a fucked up thing to do. He was asking me to lose my son. To just give him up like I was abandoning a puppy. Shit, I couldn't even abandon a puppy.

"Then he comes up to me and looks me right in the eye and says that after himself, Freddie would be next. 'Do you want to bury your son?' he asks me.

"At the time, I felt he was right. But I also hoped that he was wrong. I asked Ray what he was going to do with Freddie. He wouldn't tell me. It's best that I don't know. Thinking about the future. So Ray grabbed Freddie from the closet, and they left in his car.

"I called the police. I told them that someone broke into my home and killed my husband. I completely forgot Freddie and how he fit in the situation. When the police asked me where my son was I told them the truth. I didn't know. They just assumed that he was kidnapped. At first they thought Danny killed himself, but then I gave them a description of the person who killed him. It was obviously fake, but I did give them a real name. I gave them the business card and told them that Doctor Tarallab killed Danny.

"The police never found Dr. Tarallab. I didn't think they would. They couldn't find Freddie either. It didn't help that we never got his prints registered. That was Danny's idea. Kinda weird, it's like Danny knew that something like this was going to happen.

"After that night I never heard from Ray again either. I hoped he was with Freddie, that they were together and safe. The police searched for Ray also, thinking he was involved with Danny's murder. Huh, they even thought that we were lovers or something, and Freddie was really Ray's child and that he kidnapped him. Real crazy shit people can come up with, sometimes crazier than the truth."

* * *

Tanya sat back and wiped the silent tears from her eyes. Belinda reached out and took her hand.

"In many ways he turned out great," Belinda said. "Although your plan didn't turn out as you hoped. They found him. From what Daryl told me, they've been with him since they placed him in the orphanage. I think he saw them before that, he just didn't remember."

"I guess you can't stop fate, huh."

"It has nothing to do with fate. What Daryl, Freddie, was going though was going to happen to him because that is who they are. I don't know, maybe they have to go through this for some higher purpose. Why them? Why do they see these Beings? I think that they are meant to stop them or else why do they see them?"

Belinda noticed Tanya looking past her shoulder. Tanya then took a deep breath and stretched out a bit. "Mind if I get a smoke?"

Belinda thought that that was a weird question for the moment, but said, "Sure."

Tanya smiled and left the booth. Belinda turned and watched her leave the diner. Her eyes glanced at the window where she expected to see Tanya light up, but instead she saw the homeless man. He cold-stared at Belinda and then walked away from the glass.

"What the fuck?" she whispered.

The homeless guy pissed her off. He was real and somehow part of what was going on. Belinda stepped out of the booth and walked to the window. Moving around an empty table, Belinda looked out at the parking lot. He wasn't around.

"You okay?"

It was Tanya. She stood next to her.

"Yeah, I thought I saw someone I knew."

"Oh," Tanya flinched. "Well I have to get home. I, uh, know someone who might be able to help us."

"Oh, yeah. Who?"

"I'd rather not say right now. He's kinda a recluse so I need to talk to him first."

"Okay. When can I see you again?"

"Later tonight. Maybe midnight?"

"Okay. Morbid, but okay."

"I'll come to your motel," Tanya offered.

"I don't mind coming to you."

"No. You can't. My, uh, husband will be home. It's easier for me to sneak out to see you."

"He doesn't sound like a great guy. How did you get stuck with him?"

"He kinda pushed himself into my life. He's very observant. He watches my every move, okay? So I'll come to you."

Belinda shrugged.

"Okay. Room 16. Planet Motel"

"Great," Tanya said.

They stood there for an awkward moment. They both felt they should do something. Belinda made the first move and hugged her. Tanya hugged back.

"Freddie is such a lucky man to have you," Tanya said.

Belinda smiled, touched.

"Midnight, then." Tanya released her and left, wiping her eyes with her sleeve.

* * *

Back at the motel, Belinda had a few hours to kill. She called the hospital. Visiting hours were over so she connected with the nursing station. Daryl's condition was the same.

She then stretched out on the bed and watched T.V. Belinda watched the last half of "Almost Famous" on HBO. When that was done, the station announced "Cabin Boy." Belinda changed the channel. She stopped on a local channel and watched the news. She started to doze until an entertainment segment started a story that caught her attention.

"A shadow fell across the literary world earlier today," the newscaster announced. "Ellen West, best-selling horror author of the novels 'Dove Story' and 'Mystery Run,' died. Ms. West was found in her New York apartment bedroom by a friend. Police reported that she died from a self-inflicted gunshot wound.

"In the music world..."

Belinda could not believe it.

"When it rains, it fuckin' pours," she said.

* * *

Belinda woke up. She turned to the digital clock by the bed. It was 12:32 A.M. Tanya was late.

"Shit."

She sat on the edge of the bed and rubbed her eyes. A clicking caught her attention. It was coming from the door. The knob twisted from the other side.

Belinda moved to her jacket resting on a chair and took the knife out of the inside pocket. She walked to the door and peaked out the peephole. The view was black. Whoever was out there had their hand over it.

"Tanya," Belinda called out.

The knob stopped shaking, then started up again. Someone banged on the door.

Fucker must be ramming his body against it, she thought.

Belinda noticed the door loosening from the threshold. She then went to the corner, next to the hinges, and pressed her body close. Belinda held the knife in her hand, pointing it in front of her.

The door busted open, but the chain stopped it from going further. The intruder rammed it again. The chain snapped, and the door flew open, boxing Belinda into the corner.

She heard the intruder enter and walk around the room, panting, searching. Footsteps carefully moved to the door. The panting stopped in front of her; the door placed between them.

All was quiet.

The door swung open, revealing Belinda to the intruder and the intruder to Belinda. It was the homeless guy.

With the knife gripped in her hand, Belinda punched him in the nose.

The homeless guy grabbed his bleeding nose and stumbled away from Belinda. She then moved to the desk and picked up the chair. She swung it at him, hoping to break it over his head, but the homeless guy just fell to the floor and the chair stayed in one piece. Belinda dropped the chair and stood over his body. The homeless guy laid still, possibly unconscious.

"I knew you were real, asshole."

Belinda kneeled down next to him.

"Let's see who the fuck you are."

Belinda patted his body down, searching for a wallet or something. She found nothing; the guy had nothing, not even a weapon. She decided to check his back pockets. She placed her hands under his leg and arm and flipped him over.

The homeless guy elbowed her in the jaw.

Belinda fell back on her butt, dropping the knife and grabbing her face.

The homeless guy sat up. They both looked at the knife a few feet away from them and moved to it. Homeless guy beat her to it and wrapped his hand around the handle. Before he could turn around, Belinda jumped on his back and grabbed his armed hand. She banged his fist on the floor, trying to shake it loose from his tight grip. Belinda then punched him in the bottom right of his back. The homeless man screamed out in pain and released the knife.

Belinda jumped off, pointing the knife at him. She expected the homeless guy to get up and charge her, but the blow to the back kept him down. He moaned in pain.

"Get up," Belinda ordered.

The homeless guy noisily turned on his back. "I can't," he said.

"Yes, you can, or I'm gonna stab ya."

The homeless guy blurted out a laugh through his pain. The laugh sounded familiar to her, like Daryl was laughing.

"Who are you?" she asked.

"Oh, man," he exhaled. "I'm Ray Shields."

* * *

Belinda made an icepack with a shower cap from the bathroom and some ice from the ice machine in front of the motel office. She passed it to Ray Shields. He sat in a chair with his back straight and tender. Ray pressed the icepack to his blood-clotted nose.

"Thanks," he said.

"How do I know you're telling me the truth," Belinda asked.

"Well, I don't carry any I.D. with me. That would be stupid."

"Fine, then maybe I should call the cops. I'm sure they would be interested why you broke into my room and attacked me."

Belinda walked to the phone.

Ray reached his hand out to her, setting off pain in his back. "Owe. Fuck. Wait."

Belinda turned with the phone posed in her hand to Ray.

"Well," she said.

"I left you the clue. Shit, it was the answer to where Freddie came from."

"What clue?"

Ray exhaled, annoyed.

"The clue in your apartment."

She still didn't know.

"The writing on the wall. Ring a bell?" Ray asked.

"Wait a second. Daryl wrote that on the wall."

"Yes he did, in a sense. I helped him," Ray explained.

"You were in our apartment? Why didn't Daryl tell me about it?"

"I wasn't in the apartment. I was in his head while he was sleepwalking and I wrote the words on the wall for him."

Belinda sat on the bed and relaxed in defeat.

"Jesus. I don't believe this."

"Can I explain it to you? Please? Can I?"

"Yeah, go," Belinda urged. "It better be good."

"Okay. After I took Freddie, Daryl, away I drove him back to my place and made him look different. I dyed his hair; cut it shorter, even smeared dirt on him to make it look like he was away from home for a long time. I even stole some clothes that I knew his mother would never let him wear and put them on him. I then drove to the train yard in Farmingdale. I placed him on an empty train car. I had no idea where it was going. I didn't want to know, you see. It was all for his benefit. So I sat in the car and waited for the train to leave, making sure that no one found him, hoping that the amnesia would last long enough."

"But the Beings still found him," Belinda pointed out.

"Yeah, I'm getting to that.

"So, I hid out in the pine Barrens. You know, where the Jersey Devil is supposed to be."

Belinda shrugged her shoulders, not knowing what he was talking about.

Ray sighed.

"Okay," he continued. "I came back to Owel a few years ago. I was worried about Tanya. I had this feeling that something was going down. And something did. I followed her home one day and saw that she was living with some guy."

"Her new husband," Belinda said.

"Shit, did she tell you that? That guy is not her husband. He's Dr. Tarallab."

"The guy who was treating your brother. Why would she marry a guy who was involved in her husband's murder? It doesn't make sense."

"Okay, first off, Tarallab is not a doctor. He's not even human," Ray said.

"Oh, please."

"I'd never seen Tarallab before that time, or at least, I thought I didn't. While I was in the Barrens, I had this trunk that belonged to my father. There were pictures and journals by our family. Most of these pictures were of the Beings in their good and demonic forms, but there were some of this one human being who was kind of hanging in the background. A man was mentioned in the journals. Mostly he was just referred to as a man, but there were times when he was mentioned by name: Labaralt, Ballarat, Labralat, Tarallab. When I remembered the picture and saw him at Tanya's house, I put it together. This guy in her house is Tarallab or whoever the fuck he calls himself."

"Okay, so if what you're saying is true, then this guy's family has been killing off men in your family-"

"No!" Ray said. "You're not listening. It is the same guy. No child can look the same as the father. Genetically, it is possible. The wife or mother mixes the pot. It is the same guy."

"Let's say that this is true," Belinda said. "Then what is he doing with Tanya?"

"I think he came back and forced himself into her life. He's waiting."

"For Daryl."

"Exactly."

"Is he related to the Beings? Does he control them or something?"

"Not exactly. Let me get back on track here. So, I stayed in Owel, found an old house in the woods and made that my home.

"One day I was in the diner that Tanya worked in. She wasn't there, which I knew, I didn't want to get her attention yet. I sat at a booth and ate breakfast while these two kids were talking. They were arguing about the artistic validity of 'The Michelina Show' and how it was going to transfer to a Saturday morning cartoon."

"Michelina was your cat."

"Hey, how did you know that?"

"Tanya told me."

"Yeah, I loved that cat. I had to give her away to a friend of mine when I left town. It sucked.

"Anyway, the kids talked about Daryl Hersh and his mysterious past. He was found on a train and had amnesia. When the kids left I turned around and saw that they left the magazine behind. It was opened to the article and had a picture of Daryl. He had Freddie's face, but older.

"From there I did some research and tracked him down to New York. So I felt that I could now help him. I found out where you lived and I did this trick."

"What trick?" Belinda asked.

"I put myself into his head."

"What? Like magic?"

"Don't look at me like that."

"Okay, go on."

"I went in his head while he was sleepwalking," Ray continued. "It seemed to be his most vulnerable time. I wrote the words Owel Danny Shields on the wall."

"You say it so naturally as if it was so easy to do."

"Everybody has the capability of magic. What? You think I did it right the first shot? It took me weeks to do. It was common in our family. My grandfather's journal mentioned how he was able to project himself all over the world. His brother was able to read minds. I guess we're from special blood, or something."

"Uh, huh."

"Freddie has this in him as well. What? Stop looking at me like that."

"This is crazy," Belinda stated. She then looked at her watch. "Where's Tanya?"

"She said she would be here at midnight."

"How do you know that?"

"I talked to her at the diner tonight. You know, when she was talking to you."

"What did she say to you?"

"She said how glad she was to see me and how something bad was happening with Freddie. She told me who you were; stuff I already knew. Then she asked for my help and wanted me to meet her here at midnight."

"So you broke in."

"Hey. I thought Tarallab followed her here and you two were in trouble," Ray said. "I came to rescue you, and then you attack me."

"You could have just told me who you were back in New York."

"Please, you weren't ready yet," he said. "You want to help Freddie you're going to have to stop looking at me like some psycho and open your mind a bit. We're dealing with an evil that has been with my family for years."

"You think it can be stopped?" Belinda asked.

"No."

"So Daryl is fucked."

"Not necessarily. I beat them, I'm still here."

"You don't see the Beings anymore?"

"Oh, I still see them. We're very close, but I'm not about to shoot myself because of them."

"I don't understand."

"Of course you don't. You're not ready yet."

Belinda, getting tired of Ray, sat up and walked to the window.

"Listen, maybe we should find Tanya," Belinda offered.

"You mean go to her house?"

"Yeah."

"Tarallab could be there."

She turned to him. "Then she could be in danger."

She watched him. Ray looked frightened.

"Well," Belinda urged. "If she's in trouble we have to go help her."

"Fine. Let's go."

* * *

They drove in Belinda's car to Tanya's house. She parked it across the street and studied the house. It was dark, deserted. The whole street looked empty. Belinda assumed that it was due to the late hour and all the residents were sleeping.

"Do you have a weapon?" Belinda asked Ray.

"No, but if what I think is in there, then weapons aren't going to be any good."

"So, my knife is useless. This whole situation is useless," Belinda said, starting to lose the rest of her patience. "We might as well go home and wait for everybody to die."

"Cool it, would ya," Ray said with his hands up in surrender. "It might slow them down."

"Them? I thought it's just Tarallab in there."

"Tarallab is a collective of a whole. Kinda like your band. The so-called doctor is a front man of sorts. The rest of the band is in there with him."

"Great."

Belinda exited the car and made her way across the street, determined. Ray chased after her, paranoid of his environment.

"Hey, hey. What are you doing?" Ray shushed after her.

She walked and said, "Going in the house."

"Through the front door?"

"Yep."

"Jesus. Where did you buy your balls?"

Belinda stopped at the door. Ray stood next to her. She opened the storm door and rested it on her shoulder. She turned the knob. It was locked.

"Oh, well," Ray said.

"I get the impression you don't want to be here. I thought you beat this guy Tarallab at his own game?"

"I did, but it doesn't mean 'he' can't physically kill me."

Belinda had no idea what he meant by that, but she didn't pursue it. She wanted to find Tanya.

Belinda walked to the large window in front of the house and pressed herself between the shrubs that lined the side of the house. She cupped her hands on the glass and peaked in. Belinda saw very little through the thin curtain.

"So what are we going to do?" Ray asked. He hopped around from foot to foot like an addict.

Belinda turned and noticed Ray's nervous dance.

"Relax, Tom Arnold," she said.

Belinda looked at the ground and spotted a large rock. She picked it up.

"What are you going to do with that?" Ray asked.

Belinda threw it at close range through the window. It left a large hole, but not large enough for them to crawl through.

"Jesus fuck," Ray whispered.

Belinda took out her knife and started chiseling the edges of broken glass, making the hole bigger. She then peaked into the darkness of the house and called out Tanya's name.

No answer.

"You could have picked a less conspicuous window," Ray said, looking around the street. "I wouldn't be surprised if the cops came by."

"It's okay. We're family," Belinda explained.

Two arms reached out of the window from inside the house and grabbed Belinda's hand.

"Ray!" she called out.

Ray saw the arms and said, "Jesus."

The brown, saggy arms pulled at Belinda, digging black nails into her skin. They played a game of tug of war using Belinda's arm as a rope.

"What the fuck is it," she whimpered.

"Just pull!"

The arms gave a sharp tug, pulling Belinda from Ray's grip and into the house.

* * *

Slightly upside down, Belinda flew across the living room and into the wall. She landed on the floor as framed pictures fell on her back.

Dazed, Belinda brought her head up and looked at her attacker. It stood over seven feet tall on four legs. It was huge, hulking, nothing at all like the Beings. The creature made its way towards Belinda.

Panicky, Belinda jumped on her feet and gripped the knife in her hand. "C'mon, fuck face," she said, gathering her courage.

The creature opened its arms and released a roar from its fanged mouth, revealing rocks for teeth, completely vicious.

"Fuck!"

Belinda charged.

The creature picked Belinda up and lifted her off the ground. Belinda screamed and stabbed at its head. The penetration unfazed the creature until she popped its amber eye.

The creature released her. Belinda dropped to the floor and landed on her feet.

While the creature held its punctured eye and stumbled around the room, Belinda took her chance. She drove the knife into the creature's belly. It screamed and reached for Belinda. She jerked her body away from it and stabbed it again and again and again. The creature stood and held its belly wound while sludge slopped out of it. It started to waiver, getting weaker. The legs buckled and the creature fell to the floor.

"Holy shit," Belinda whispered, relieved, catching her breath.

"Is it safe?"

Belinda shook her head and cleaned the knife blade on the back of the sofa.

"Yeah."

Ray entered through the window and looked at the creature.

"My God."

"Yeah, thanks for your help," Belinda said.

"Hey, I didn't beat Tarallab to get killed by...by...fuck I don't even know what to call that thing."

Belinda, pissed with Ray, turned and faced the back of the house. There was a kitchen and, next to that, a hall.

"Tanya," she called out.

No answer.

Belinda peaked into the kitchen. She tried the lights but they didn't work. She then walked down the hall.

Ray looked at the creature on the floor.

"Uh, Belinda," he said.

Belinda opened a door in the hall and found the bathroom. It was unoccupied.

"Yeah, Ray?"

"This thing is moving."

She stepped out into the hall and looked at him. "What do you mean? Is it alive?"

Ray backed away from it.

"No," he said. "Its belly is moving."

"Shit," Belinda said.

She walked over and stood next to Ray. Belinda watched the body. The belly rippled as if it had severe indigestion.

"What's it doing Ray?"

"How the fuck should I know."

"You're the mystical expert here. You're supposed to have the answers."

A little claw popped out of the creature's belly wound, then another. The two tiny arms ripped the wound wider, giving way for a head. It was a mini version of the creature. A baby. The thing squeezed its way out of the belly and rolled to the floor.

Then, another came out.

"I don't like this," Belinda said.

They backed away.

Ten creatures popped out, cleaning and biting themselves. They turned to Belinda and Ray at the mouth of the hall and awkwardly moved after them.

Belinda and Ray ran down the hall and stopped at the last door. It was locked.

"Shit, help me with this," she said.

The creatures moved closer, releasing baby roars of anger.

Belinda and Ray rammed the locked door. It opened and they fell into the room. They quickly went to a dresser against the wall and moved it in front of the door.

As they caught their breath, Belinda's cell phone rang.

"C'mon, man," she said.

Belinda was about to answer it when Ray caught her attention and pointed into the room. Tanya was on the bed with her limbs tied with entrails to the bedpost and a chunk of meat gagged in her mouth. Tanya looked at them and tried to speak though the flesh in her mouth. They went over and cut her loose with Belinda's knife. Ray took the meat out of her mouth.

"Are you all right?" Belinda asked her.

Tanya spit blood out. "Yeah, I think so."

The barricaded door started to rattle.

"Is Tarallab here?" Ray asked Tanya.

"No, I don't think so," Tanya said, rubbing her wrists. "He left a few hours ago. I don't know, but I think he was scared about something."

There was a loud cracking at the door. They all turned to it and saw little claws breaking through the dresser and pulling the wood apart.

"We have to go," Belinda stated.

Belinda picked up a large lamp and drove it through the bedroom window.

"Hey, that opens you know," Tanya said.

"Girl has some anger issue," Ray offered.

They went out through the window and ran to Belinda's car. Loaded and ready in the vehicle, Belinda drove them away from the house.

Ray turned to Tanya in the back seat. "Are you really okay? Did he hurt you?"

"No. I'm surprised, too. He found out that you were in town, Belinda. I thought he would go crazy or something. He locked me up and said he was going to wait for you to come to him."

"So that big thing in your living room wasn't Tarallab?" Belinda asked.

Tanya shrugged. "I have no idea what you're talking about. I didn't see anything but Tarallab."

"He probably left it there to kill us," Ray offered. "He didn't say where he went," Ray asked Tanya.

Tanya shrugged her shoulders.

Belinda remembered her phone call and took out her cell phone. She checked the last incoming call and saw that it was the hospital. Belinda pulled the car over on the side of a neighborhood street.

"What is it?" Ray asked.

Belinda ignored him and dialed the hospital. A nurse picked up.

"Hi. This is Belinda Hersh. You just called me."

"Yes, Mrs. Hersh. I'm afraid we have some...troubling news."

"Oh, God. Daryl's dead?" Belinda asked.

Ray looked at Tanya who covered her mouth in a gasp.

"No. We don't think so," the nurse said. "Daryl's gone. He left his room."

VI

Lurgee

Daryl and Freddie broke into Daryl's apartment. It was late at night, getting closer to dawn. Daryl wore a powder blue pair of pants and shirt that he stole from the hospital laundry room. Freddie wanted to get started on their journey home, but Daryl insisted that he get a change of clothes and some money.

Daryl walked through the dark living room and turned on the lamp by the couch.

"Belinda, you home," Daryl called out. He checked the bedroom. It was deserted. Daryl felt relieved that Belinda wasn't back from her tour. He wasn't ready to face her, much less her new boyfriend...in the bed...together...

Daryl went back to the living room and saw Freddie looking around.

"I'm gonna do a few things, okay?" asked Daryl.

The boy nodded his head, studying a coffee table book of Michelina sketches.

"This cat looks like my uncles cat," Freddie observed. "Even has the same name."

Daryl ignored him, heading for the bedroom.

He changed into a pair of jeans and a flannel shirt. Daryl sat on the edge of the bed and slipped on a pair of black work shoes. He then looked around the room. It was no different than the way he saw it last. Daryl noticed all the little details that were in the duplicate room back at the Clinic were in their right place. The items from the Clinic were copies, he figured. Did Belinda help them design the room? Why would she?

Depressed, Daryl walked over to the dresser and picked up his wallet. He only had a few dollars, but he also had a credit card. He slipped it into his back pocket and left the room.

Freddie kneeled down in front of the television and watched the video that Kate made of Daryl sleepwalking.

"What are you watching that for," he asked the boy.

"I've never seen how it affected me before," Freddie said. "You look so happy when they're around."

Daryl kneeled down next to Freddie and asked, "You see them, too?"

"Yes. They are so beautiful. They make me feel so safe and...loved. 'Specially when it feels like there's no one left in the world that does love me."

"Yeah, well, that's all gonna change when you get older."

"Look," Freddie said, pointing to the screen. "Look at how great it is. How could that turn bad?"

Daryl released a tired and frustrated sigh.

"I don't know, Freddie."

"Think."

"Shouldn't we be going?"

"Yes, I guess so," Freddie said, saddened.

"So where do we go?"

Freddie pointed at the writing on the wall.

"There," the boy stated.

"What? Owel?"

"Yes."

"That's where you're from?"

"Yes."

"Listen," Daryl said. "Do you know who this name is next to it?"

"Danny Shields," Freddie said. "He was my father."

"Oh. Where is he?"

"He's dead."

"I'm sorry."

Freddie nodded.

"I just need my coat and then we can go," Daryl said, trying to lighten the mood. "Okay?"

* * *

Tanya sat in the back of Belinda's rent-a-car. She didn't know how to take the news about her son. The good part: he was out of the coma; the bad part: no one knew where he was.

From her diagonal position in the back of the car, Tanya was able to see Belinda's face. Belinda drove the car but her face revealed that her mind was somewhere else. Belinda bit her lip right after her jaw started to jiggle. Tanya could tell her daughter-in-law was holding back tears. She envied and felt sorry for Belinda.

Tanya blocked the bad from her head. She tried to think positive thoughts. Freddie will be found, she believed, and everything will be how it was supposed to be. Although, Danny would not be there to share it with her.

"Where are you when I need you," Tanya whispered to herself.

Ray turned from the front seat. "What was that?"

"Hm?"

"I thought you said something."

"Oh, no."

Ray turned back around and continued giving Belinda directions to his house.

Tanya felt glad that Ray was back. Everything she lost was trying to reunite with her. She then remembered Belinda's pregnancy. Tanya smiled, thinking about the grandchild that was on its way.

"What are you thinking about?" Belinda asked.

Belinda looked at her through the rearview mirror, catching her smile.

"About my grandchild," Tanya said.

Ray looked at Belinda, surprised.

"You're pregnant?" he asked.

"Yeah, about a month and a half now," Belinda stated.

Tanya noticed the troubled look on Ray's face. So did Belinda.

"Why?" Belinda asked Ray.

"Nothing," he said.

"Well, if you're thinking of proposing adoption or kidnapping the baby, I strongly suggest you get it out of your system. That route failed," Belinda stressed.

"Fuck you," Ray shot back. "I was just trying to do what was best for Fred."

"Oh, sure. What he needed was to be abandoned. He sure as hell didn't need someone there for him. He went through life not able to count on anyone. Daryl was dropped without help. He had no idea what was going on, and it deeply affected his life. It left him alone and depressed. And whom do you think fixed that up? Hm? Yeah, me. I didn't run from Daryl. I didn't leave and, as simple as that idea may seem, it was the hardest thing in my life to do. You took the easy way out."

Ray sat and sulked.

Tanya looked down, feeling hallow and dazed.

"You're right," Tanya said. "I should have done something. Something more."

Belinda opened her mouth to say something, but then kept it shut. Tanya remained quiet, as did Ray.

After ten minutes, Ray said, "Turn right here."

* * *

Belinda drove the car up to Ray's house; shack was more like it. It was practically dilapidated. She seriously doubted that he was paying for it. It reminded Belinda of the cabin from "The Evil Dead" movies but smaller.

"Leave your lights on a bit," Ray said.

Ray left the car and stood in front of the headlights. He took a ring of keys out of his pocket and picked a key. Ray walked to the door, unlocked it, and entered the cabin.

"What does he need a lock for? I doubt he has anything of value to steal," Belinda said.

"Ray was always a bit weird," Tanya explained. "He finds value in the simplest things."

Belinda saw a subtle candlelight glow out of the windows. Ray stood by the door and waved them in. Belinda turned off the lights and walked with Tanya to the cabin.

Like the outside, there was not much to the inside. The walls and roof seemed solid. There was a used couch across from the door. In the corner, a few sleeping bags that looked very new and next to them were a few milk crates that acted as shelves for some canned and dry foods. Ray also had some dented pots and pans. To the right side of the room was a closed door.

"We should get some sleep," Ray said. "Who wants the couch?"

"You take it," Belinda said to Tanya.

"No, you," Tanya said. "Medical reasons."

"Thanks."

Belinda sat on the couch while Tanya positioned herself on top of a sleeping bag.

"So what's next, Ray?" Belinda asked.

"I'm, uh, gonna try and find Fred."

"That teleport thing?" Belinda asked with a trace of mock.

Ray gave her a dirty look and entered the other room.

"Hey, what if we have to use the bathroom," Belinda called after him.

"T.P. on the top shelf. Just pick a tree," he said, closing the door behind him.

Belinda and Tanya looked at each other with raised eyebrows.

"Eiw," they said in unison.

They lay back on their substitute beds, making themselves comfortable.

"Do you really believe that shit about trying to get into Daryl's head?" Belinda asked.

"Let's just say I have more faith in Ray than God," Tanya responded.

Belinda left it at that. She stretched out on the couch. It smelled like a wet dog, but she fell asleep.

* * *

At Newark Penn Station (by way of the Path train), Daryl paid for two bus tickets on his credit card. When Daryl motioned to Freddie at his side, the attendant looked at the empty space, then looked at Daryl oddly.

"Sure, man. Two tickets to Aldrich Road in Owel," the attendant said.

They had a few hours to kill so they went to the McDonald's by the terminal and ate breakfast. Daryl asked Freddie what he wanted. The boy said, nothing. He was not hungry.

"You have to eat, kid," Daryl said. "I've been out of the Clinic as long as you and I'm starving."

"I don't need food," Freddie responded.

Whatever, Daryl thought.

He ordered a large meal and hoped the boy would see the food and spike up an appetite.

They sat by the window and looked out for their bus.

"You think they're looking for us?" Daryl asked the boy.

"Who?"

"Dr. Ballarat. The Clinic. The police."

Freddie sadly shook his head.

"No. I don't think so. Although, Ballarat might want to know where you are."

"I was thinking I should call him."

"Why?"

"To let him know that I'm okay and that I'll be back in a few days once we get you home."

"Daryl, you can't go back once you go through the green door."

"Freddie, I have to go back."

"You can't go back. It is gone. It never existed," Freddie stated.

"Then what about you?" Daryl asked. "Are you not real as well?"

Freddie remained silent.

"I was this close to getting better," Daryl muttered.

"Yes. Then Kate stopped you. Do you know why?"

"You said to bring you home."

"Yes and no." Freddie released a breath. "Daryl, Ballarat wants to harm you."

"You just told me that the Clinic doesn't exist, but Ballarat does."

Freddie brooded.

"He's the first doctor that truly understands what I'm going through," Daryl said. "He wants me to get better and he knows how to get me better."

"He killed my father," Freddie stated.

Daryl saw the sadness in the boy's face. It depressed him. He looked away and scanned the dining area. Daryl noticed a few people looking at him oddly as if Daryl was talking to himself. He ignored them and turned back to Freddie.

"I'm sorry, Fred," Daryl said, "but you might..."

"My father was a patient of his many years ago. He thought he was being helped, but it was a trick. Ballarat wanted him dead."

"Why? Why would he do that? What does Ballarat have to gain with your father's death?"

"I don't know."

Daryl patiently nodded his head.

Freddie shot Daryl an angry face.

"What?" Freddie asked. "You don't believe me."

"I just don't think you know the whole story. You might be making connections to bits of fact. You know what I mean?"

"You're looking down at me. Why? Because I'm a kid. It is not me who doesn't have the whole story, Daryl."

Daryl shrugged his shoulders. Freddie sat back in the chair and crossed his arms, sulking. Daryl continued to eat, moving the food closer and closer to the boy, hoping he would have a bite. He didn't.

* * *

Belinda woke up on the couch. She looked at her watch; it was almost 2 P.M. Tanya slept in the sleeping bag, looking peaceful and quiet. Belinda stood up and stretched her arms and legs. She wandered around, looking at the woods through the window, yawning.

Turning back to the room behind her, she spotted a trunk. Belinda quietly walked over to it and opened the lid. Inside she found stacks of papers and bound journals held together by rubber bands. It belonged to Daryl's grandfather; the one Ray mentioned, she assumed. A collection of the family curse.

Belinda sat in front of the trunk and took out a few bundles. She took a rubber band off one collection of pictures and looked through them. They were mostly of the Beings, sketched in the same style as Daryl's hand. Some of them were dated a hundred years ago.

A sketch caught her attention. It was a Being in a bedroom. It was vicious, floating out of the wall, trying to reach out of the paper. Belinda looked past the Being and noticed someone in the closet, hiding in the shadows. It was a man, smiling. He looked handsome as if he belonged in a commercial. It had to be Tarallab. As Belinda continued to flip through the pictures, she noticed that Tarallab hid in many sketches. He smiled in all of them, enjoying himself.

She placed the sketches back and picked up the journals. Belinda opened one, making the spine crack. She flipped through the pages, noticing the dates on the entries. The one she held in her hand was written in 1901.

A picture drawn in the journal made her stop. It was a sketch of the four-legged creature from Tanya's house. Belinda went to the beginning of the entry and read:

Something different happened last night, something scary and... A sound from downstairs awoke me from my bed. I saw Naja sleeping next to me and knew it wasn't one of the Beings because they always showed themselves to me, eventually playing hide and seek games. I guessed that there could be a prowler in the house. I reached under the bed and unlocked my box and loaded my service revolver. I checked the children's rooms and saw them deep in sleep. I then went downstairs and peaked into the family room. I kept the light off, not wanting the prowler to know I was in the room. After a moment of silence and inspection, I started to doubt what I heard. I stepped deeper into the room and announced who I was, that I'm a police officer and that I was armed. I still didn't get a response. So I searched the room, the kitchen, the doors, every nook and cranny of the lower part of the house. There was no sign of a break in. No one was around, but I felt like there was...a presence. I was standing by the stairs and about to go back to bed when I heard a growling. I quickly turned around and saw a...thing. I never saw anything like it in my life. It grabbed me and pressed me to the wall. I fought and struggled; I was so frightened. Just as I was about to fire my revolver at the creature, it bit me. The creature bit the hand that I held the gun in, making me drop it. The gun hit the floor and a shot went off. The next thing I remembered was Naja and the children kneeling around me. I was on the steps. I felt like I just woke up. But it wasn't a dream because the bite on my hand was there. Naja wanted to call for help, but I told her not to. How was I gonna explain to my superiors that we had a break-in with no visible sign of a break-in, and that a creature with four legs bit my hand? I told her that we were going to deal with this ourselves. She complied and helped me clean up. I reassured the children that there really wasn't a monster in the house and I just cut my hand while I was sleeping. They seemed satisfied, but I didn't underestimate them. My children are very smart. So today I have this bite. It stopped bleeding, and I hope it heals. But most importantly, I hope that it didn't give me some disease, like a wild dog would or a snake.

Belinda read a few more entries from the journal. It was all standard for her. The Beings turned into demons and tormented the writer.

She then remembered Daryl's bite.

Belinda picked up a few more journals by different authors and skimmed them, searching. They all mention a change, a creature biting them, a bite that did not heal.

A rejuvenating energy picked Belinda up off the floor. She entered the room where Ray slept.

* * *

Daryl sat on the bus heading to Aldrich Road. He slept in a seat with his head resting on the window in the middle of the bus. Freddie sat next to him, satisfied with an aisle seat. The boy was still angry with Daryl.

There were a few other passengers on the bus. A girl in her early twenties sat in the back with a carry-on bag so stuffed it looked ready to burst from the seams. She read a paperback, minding her own business. An old couple sat in the front, constantly reminding the driver that they wanted to get off at Old Bridge. The driver promised he would stop there, trying to hold a smile.

When the bus exited the Parkway and entered Route 9, Daryl broke from his sleep, and saw the Beings floating above the seats, slowly moving towards him. Panicky, Daryl turned to Freddie, but the boy was gone. He looked back at the evil Beings. They floated right at his face. Daryl screamed out.

The bus stopped.

Daryl pushed himself into the seat, kicking his legs and waving off the Beings.

Someone grabbed his wrist.

Daryl punched the attacker. His fist connected with a skin-padded skull, popping the knuckles in his fingers.

"God damn!"

Daryl opened his eyes. The Beings were gone. He looked out the window. The bus was parked on the side of the road. He turned to the inside of the bus. The old couple in the front stared at him, frightened of his next move. The girl in the back stood up, ready for a fight. The bus driver stood in the seat across from Daryl and held his jaw.

"What...what happened?" Daryl asked.

"You went crazy," the driver said. "Just started screaming and flipping out."

Daryl looked in the seat next to him.

"Where's Freddie?" he asked.

The driver looked at Daryl cautiously.

"Listen, I'm not going to get into this again with you. There is no boy. It's just you. You can redeem that other ticket in Toms River."

Daryl laughed. He felt thoroughly embarrassed. He saw their eyes watching, preparing for another freak out.

"I should go," Daryl said. "I'm sorry I hit you."

"Hey, you want me to call an ambulance?" the driver asked.

Daryl remained silent. He left the bus. He stepped out onto the side of the road and started walking south. After a few feet, he stopped and flipped out as the traffic passed him. He kicked his legs and threw his arms and screamed, "Fuck!"

"You shouldn't use language like that," Freddie said. He stood next to Daryl.

"Where were you?"

"I'm a child. You shouldn't use language like that," he said.

Freddie walked away, heading south.

"Hey, where are you going?" he called out after him.

Freddie kept walking and yelled out, "Home."

Daryl reluctantly followed.

* * *

"Tanya, wake up."

Belinda stood above her, looking scared.

"What is it?" Tanya asked.

"It's Ray. Something is wrong with him."

Tanya followed Belinda into the other room. Ray lay on top of a bald mattress. His body stiffened and his limbs jerked up and down. His eyes were open, but he looked at nothing.

They kneeled around him.

"What should we do?" Belinda asked.

Tanya shrugged her shoulders; she had no idea what to do. She touched Ray's chest with her finger. "Ray, wake up."

He kept going.

Belinda looked at her. "Should we call an ambulance?"

"Shit, I don't know," Tanya said. She then grabbed her brother-in-law by the shoulders and shook his torso. "Ray!"

He screamed and flailed his arms.

Belinda and Tanya fell backwards, avoiding his limbs, and landed on their asses.

Ray sat up, awakening and catching his breath. He noticed Belinda and Tanya staring at him.

"Are you okay?" Tanya asked.

"Yeah, what are you two doing?"

"I came in to talk to you, and I found you having some kind of attack," Belinda explained.

"I was?" Ray looked confused. "I was channeling. I was in Freddie's head, but I got...pushed out."

"By who?" Belinda asked.

"The Beings."

"Well, what did you see before that?" Tanya asked. "Is he okay?"

"I think so," Ray said. "I saw a view from a bus. The side of the road moved by really fast."

"He's going somewhere," Tanya said.

"Yeah, but I don't know where," Ray said. "But there was something weird. Before he was on the bus, I saw him walking around the bus station."

"What's so weird about that?" Tanya asked.

"I can only enter his head when he's sleeping, usually before and after R.E.M."

"He's in a state of sleep," Tanya said. "He's sleepwalking. Is he is danger?"

"I don't know," Ray honestly said. "So why did you want to wake me?"

"I wanted to ask you about the bites," Belinda said.

"Okay."

With the expression on his face, Ray seemed to know where the conversation was going.

"The Beings turned evil after they got bitten. But what bit them looked nothing like the Beings. It was one of those four-legged things back at the house. That's why you were scared to go in the house, because if it bites you it puts the poison in you. A poison that makes you hallucinate, deforming the Beings, like a drug. They just look evil but in reality they are the same."

"Congratulations," Ray said. "You figured out how to save his life."

"So," Tanya said, "if we can make Freddie face the Beings, he will see them for who they are."

Ray nodded.

A little hope crept into Tanya.

* * *

Daryl and Freddie got on another bus at Manalapan. The bus was crowded with kids and commuters. They kept quiet and avoided suspicion. When they entered Owel, Freddie pointed out the window to Aldrich Road. Daryl signaled the driver to stop.

They stepped off and stood on the corner of Route 9 and Aldrich Road. Daryl wanted to eat. Freddie had no problem with that. They went into the Taco Bell. Daryl ate a few burritos while Freddie sat and stared out the window.

"Want something?" Daryl asked.

Freddie shook his head, avoiding Daryl's eyes.

"So, does anything seem familiar to you? Are we getting closer to your home?"

"I'm not sure," Freddie said.

Daryl left it at that.

After he ate, Freddie led Daryl down Aldrich Road. It was wooded and cold. They passed a few abandoned and occupied houses.

"You know where you're going?" Daryl asked.

"I feel it this way," Freddie responded.

They stopped at the entrance to an unnamed development. Freddie led the way in.

"I've been here before," Daryl said.

Freddie walked to his destination and said, "We're almost home."

They turned onto Tunisia Ave and walked a few blocks. Freddie and Daryl stopped at house 256.

"You live here?" Daryl asked.

"Yes."

"Are you sure? It looks deserted."

"I'm sure." The boy turned to Daryl and looked at him. "This doesn't seem familiar to you."

Daryl shook his head.

"Maybe when we get inside," Freddie said with a trace of hopefulness.

"Is your mom here?"

Freddie tilted his head, searching his thoughts.

"Not yet," he said.

Freddie took Daryl's hand and led him to the deserted house. They entered through the front door as the sun started to set.

* * *

Tanya left in Belinda's car to get Chinese food. Ray went back to bed and tried to find Daryl again. Belinda sat on the couch and read some more journals. As she closed a journal and went to put it back, her cell phone rang.

"Hey, it's me Prudee."

"What's up?" Belinda asked.

"I'm at your apartment. Something's wrong."

"What do you mean?"

"The door was busted open. It looks like you might have been robbed."

Belinda sat up straight.

"Is anything missing?"

Belinda heard Prudee ask Jess if anything was missing.

"No. Shit, I don't know," Jess said from a distance.

"Prudee, go to the bedroom," Belinda said.

"Okay. Now what?"

"I left Daryl's wallet on the dresser. Do you see it?"

"No."

"Are you sure?"

"There's no wallet there, Bel. Sorry."

"I think Daryl came home."

An idea struck Belinda's head. She hung up with Prudee and took her credit card out of her wallet. Daryl and Belinda believed that they should have only one credit card with both their names on it, keeping them out of debt. She called the customer service number and connected with an operator. There was a recent purchase for two bus tickets to Aldrich Road in N.J. made at Penn Station in Newark, N.J.

"Mother fucker!" she said triumphantly.

Who was he traveling with, she thought suddenly? Tarallab?

Tanya entered the house, carrying Chinese food. She saw the smile on Belinda's face.

"What? Good news?"

"I know where Daryl is," Belinda said.

"Where?"

Ray stormed into the room with his own accomplished look.

"I know where Freddie is," he announced.

"He's in Owel," Belinda said, smiling.

Ray frowned and asked, "How do you know that?"

"He has his wallet. He bought a ticket with our credit card."

"Oh, yeah, but do you know where in Owel he is," Ray challenged.

"He's going home," Tanya offered.

Ray deflated. "Damn."

Belinda gathered her stuff. "Let's go."

"Wait a sec," Ray said. "We just can't go there unprepared. Tarallab might be there as well."

* * *

Tanya felt nervous. Not because she was in a car on the way to being reunited with her son, not because she was about to face an ancient evil that destroyed her family and held her hostage with the hopes that her son would return, but because she was in a car that had a trunk full of firearms.

"I've collected these while staying in the Barrens," Ray said. "You'd be surprised what people throw away."

Tanya hated guns and was a little bit disturbed that Belinda liked them.

"Tanya, you didn't see that thing in your house. We shouldn't take any chances," Belinda advised.

Tanya wanted to remind them that Danny killed himself with a gun, that it made no sense to have them, but she kept her mouth shut.

The sun started to set and left a colorful darkness over Tunisia Ave. Belinda parked the car in front of house 256, and stared at it.

"Oh, shit," Belinda said.

Tanya and Ray looked with her.

"What's wrong with it?" Tanya asked.

The house looked patch-worked. It was still old but there were parts that looked new and clean, unnatural and creepy in contrast. Shrubs had dead and living branches while the door was warped with a new window and knob.

"Some parts look like the way they did when we moved in," Tanya observed. "But how can that be?"

"It's like it's stuck between the past and present," Ray added.

"Daryl must be in there," Belinda said.

They exited the car and moved to the trunk. Tanya looked around the neighborhood and saw some kids playing curb ball down the street, paying them no mind. Tanya wondered if the kids saw the house the way that it was or was it only visible to their eyes.

Belinda secretly handed Tanya a loaded revolver. She held onto the handle, not used to holding a gun, and hid it under her jacket. She watched Belinda stick a revolver in the waist of her jeans and pocket a handful of bullets. Ray tucked two revolvers in his pants and took some bullets, too. Tanya shook her head, wondering how her life came to be some kind of modern western.

"Ready?" Belinda asked them.

No, Tanya thought.

She nodded her head and said, "Yes."

Tanya followed them to the driveway. The asphalt rippled between fresh-from-the-past and cracked-in-the-present.

"You think that it's safe to step on it?" Tanya asked.

"Only one way to find out," Belinda said. She took a step on a new patch of driveway. Belinda was fine.

Tanya gathered her courage and followed Ray and Belinda to the front door.

* * *

Daryl and Freddie stepped into the house. It was dark, musty, old, and dilapidated.

"What are we doing here, Freddie?"

"None of this looks familiar to you?" the boy asked.

"No."

Freddie shook his head and turned his attention to the old television stand by the wall.

"What am I doing here? I could be back at the Clinic getting better," Daryl whined.

"This way."

Freddie walked to the back of the house and entered a hallway. Daryl reluctantly followed. He entered a master bedroom; it completely contrasted with the rest of the house. It was new and clean except for what Freddie was staring at. Over by the bed, above the headboard, was a splat pattern of blood. The boy started crying.

Daryl felt like a sap.

"I'm sorry, Freddie."

"This is where my father was killed."

Daryl wanted to ask how it happened, but stopped himself.

"He killed himself," a familiar voice said behind him.

Daryl turned to the door. Dr. Ballarat stood there with his smile, wearing a freshly pressed suit.

"Hello, Daryl," the doctor said.

Freddie scurried away from the doctor, pressing himself to a living houseplant. "Stay away from him, Daryl."

"I came to help you, Daryl," Ballarat said. "All of this is a waste of time. What does it matter that this boy gets home? He is trying to keep you sick. But, then again, maybe he just needs help. You cannot turn a child away, Daryl. But you need to be cured first. How can you help someone when you cannot help yourself? You want to be helped, don't you?"

Daryl looked in Ballarat's eyes, falling dizzy.

"Yes," Daryl said.

"Then let's get started."

Ballarat reached behind his back and took out the shotgun from the Clinic. He handed it to Daryl.

* * *

Belinda, Ray, and Tanya entered the house. The inside was just the same as the outside, flickering between two times.

"Shit hurts my eyes," Ray said, rubbing the ache in his sockets.

Tanya moved over to an end table next to the couch and turned on a new lamp. It brightened. Curious, Tanya walked over to the old television. She turned it on. Nothing happened.

"This place is out of power but the stuff that is stuck in the past has power," Tanya said.

"Freaky," Ray said.

Belinda stepped deeper into the house, making the floor creak.

Tanya moved towards her and said, "Careful."

Belinda, remembering what Susan the neighbor told her about the basement, stopped in a secure spot and called out...

* * *

"Daryl!"

"Belinda?" Daryl asked, frightened. He turned to Freddie behind him. "That sounded like Belinda."

Ballarat turned to the open door and then back to Daryl.

"Do you want to speak to her?" the doctor asked.

Daryl shook his head.

"No. Yes. I don't know."

"You think she came here to hurt you," Ballarat said. "Stop your progress."

"I...I don't know."

"She doesn't want you to get better, Daryl. She came here to keep you in torment."

Daryl hugged the shotgun, pressing it close to his beating heart. He knew Ballarat was right.

"I can't face her," Daryl said.

"I'll take care of her," Ballarat offered.

* * *

Tanya saw Tarallab enter the living room. Ray and Belinda drew their guns. The so-called doctor smiled and made eye contact with them all.

"I'm afraid he doesn't want to see any of you," Tarallab stated.

"You're him," Belinda said. "The one from the pictures."

"Him? If that is how your mind can classify me, then fine."

"Where is he?"

"He is safe. But, like me, Daryl thinks you are going to disturb his progress. He is so close to getting what he needs."

"You're going to..." Tanya began.

"Repeat the pattern," Tarallab finished. "And you three are not in it, well, except for Belinda here. We'll meet again in say...thirteen years. Then I'll get two for the price of one."

Belinda pulled the hammer back on the revolver, anger creasing her face.

Tarallab held his finger up to her. "Up, one second." He pointed to the roof.

Parts of the ceiling exploded. Three four-legged creatures fell out. One fell on Ray and took him down to the basement, breaking through the floor. One landed on the floor but fell through it, taking the surrounding floor with it, the floor that Tanya stood on, sending her down the basement on a slide. The last creature landed on its four legs, safe and secure.

"Now you may fire if you like," Tarallab said.

The creature moved towards Belinda.

* * *

"Come here, Daryl," Freddie said.

Ballarat appeared between Daryl and Freddie. The doctor took the boy and threw him in the closet. The door closed on its own, and a dresser slid in front of it, barricading Freddie in.

Ballarat smiled at Daryl.

"We don't have much time, Daryl. I think they're coming."

The doctor pointed to the wall next to the bed. Daryl saw the plaster stretch like rubber. The Beings pressed their evil faces out.

* * *

Tanya woke up on the floor of the basement. A bit of light shined down from upstairs, but not enough to make a difference. All she saw was dust and silhouettes of boxes.

She stood and looked up at the hole. Tanya saw Belinda walk backwards past the hole and a creature on four legs moving towards her. Tanya drew her gun and aimed at the thing.

Ray screamed from the dark.

She turned to the darkness behind her.

"Ray," she called out.

A creature roared.

A gun fired.

Tanya then remembered that there was another creature down there with her. She twisted around the badly lit space, searching the dusty darkness.

A pair of amber eyes glowed in the dark a few feet away from her.

Tanya fired at them.

* * *

Belinda pressed against the peeling/fresh wall. The creature watched her and drooled on the floor. It tilted its head and studied her.

"Come on. Do something," Belinda stressed.

A trace of a grin twitched on the corner of the creature's maw. It then jolted for her.

Belinda fired all six rounds into the creature's torso. It jolted back with each hit, releasing a spray of muck from its body and falling to the floor.

Dead?

* * *

Tanya checked the barrel and saw that she had four bullets left in her gun. The amber eyes disappeared. She hoped that she killed it, but Tanya didn't feel that lucky.

Ray screamed again. This time there was a crash of wood with it.

Tanya turned to the sounds.

"Ray?" she whispered.

Ray released a moan.

There was rough panting, animal-like.

From her left.

From her right.

Tanya pointed the gun and looked around. She could not see anything and it pissed her off.

Then they showed themselves, stepping into the light. Two creatures trapped Tanya.

* * *

Belinda quickly reloaded her revolver. She walked over to the body of the creature. Belinda was unsure if it was supposed to breath or not. The body lay still, and its eyes stared in one direction.

"Fuck it," she said.

Belinda walked around the creature and towards the back hall when...

The creature grabbed her leg and pulled Belinda off the floor. She landed flat on her face. The gun flew out of her hand and slid to the back glass door.

Belinda twisted her body around and tried to pull her leg from the creature's grip. It was strong. It stood on its four legs and lifted her off the floor by her ankle. It chuckled as Belinda hung upside down from its grip. She reached into her jacket and took out her knife. Belinda tried to slash at it, but the creature tossed her into the air.

She flew across the living room, into the kitchen, and landed on the sink with her hip, busting a new faucet. She dropped to the floor. A sharp pain traveled around her back as water from the broken sink rained down. She looked around for her knife; it was not around. Franticly, Belinda stood on her feet and looked through the drawers for a weapon. They were all empty.

The creature stood at the entrance of the kitchen, stepping into the water.

Belinda saw the portable television sitting on the counter. It was stuck in the past, operable. Getting an idea, Belinda turned the set on, hopped up on the counter, and smashed the T.V. on the wet floor while it remained plugged into the wall.

Electricity from the smashed television jerked the creature's body like a crazy marionette. The amber eyes rolled back and melted in the creature's sockets, releasing smoke.

The creature exploded.

Belinda closed and covered her eyes, shrinking her body back. She felt warm liquid chunks of flesh slap her body.

She opened her eyes. Creature's blood coated the room, and smoke from its singed flesh filled the air. It stunk. Chunks of the creature were strewn around. The little creatures from its belly were dead and scorched on the floor. The lower half of the body tipped over and made a splash in the water.

Belinda unplugged the television and hopped off the counter, placing her feet in the water. She left the room, picked up her revolver by the back door, and moved to the hole in the floor.

"Tanya," she called out.

* * *

Tanya fired the last of her bullets at the two creatures standing in front of her, two for each one. The creatures took the slugs with ease. Tanya started to cry.

"Oh, shit."

From out of the darkness behind the creatures, Ray sprung out and hopped on a creature's back. He pressed his gun to its head and repeatedly fired, chipping away the skull and splashing the bits of brain to the floor. The other creature moved to help its partner and tried to pull Ray off, but Ray was strong and manic.

"Tanya!"

She looked up to see Belinda poking out of the hole above. She reached her hand out to Tanya. Tanya climbed up on a box and took her daughter-in-law's hand. Belinda helped her up through the hole.

"What about Ray?" she asked when she reached the next level.

Ray and the two creatures were gone, but they heard them fighting in the dark. Belinda pointed her gun at the darkness, frustrated and hesitant.

"Shit, I don't want to hit him," Belinda said.

"Ray!" Tanya screamed.

"Get Fred!" he screamed. "Go!"

"We just can't leave him," Tanya said.

Belinda stood on her feet. Tanya could tell Belinda wanted to stay.

"He wants us to get Daryl," Belinda said. "He's trying to help us."

Tanya watched Belinda walk to the hall, her face determined. Tanya reluctantly followed her, praying for Ray.

* * *

The Beings stretched the wall, teasing and taunting him, making vicious faces. Ballarat stood next to Daryl and placed a comforting hand on his shoulder.

"It's okay, Daryl," Ballarat said. "Remember the process."

Daryl nodded his head, trying hard to swallow his fear. He squeezed his hands around the shotgun.

The bedroom door pounded.

"Daryl!" Belinda called from the other side.

Daryl, frightened, looked at the door.

"She's trying to keep you in misery, Daryl," Ballarat said.

"Daryl, let us in," Belinda screamed.

"Don't worry, Daryl. They can't get in," Ballarat assured.

* * *

Tanya and Belinda took turns ramming the door with their bodies. After a few useless slams, they stopped and rubbed the pain in their arms.

"It's like cement," Tanya said.

"There are windows, right?" Belinda asked.

"Yeah, two."

"Stay here."

Belinda left.

Tanya continued to ram the door. She said...

* * *

"Freddie, please open the door."

Daryl curiously looked at the bedroom door.

"Who was that?" he asked Ballarat.

The doctor shook his head, all innocent. "I don't know."

"It could be Freddie's mom." Daryl shook his head, trying to clear his brain. "Wait...you put Freddie in the closet."

"I had to. He was trying to stop you. He doesn't want you to get better."

"He told me that you killed his father."

Ballarat sadly smiled and said, "The little boy is confused. Yes, I knew his father. He was a patient of mine. In fact, he was one of my first that I started to treat. He was the first person that I tried Final Phase with, but he died from the side affects.

"But that was a long time ago. Final Phase works. You saw Ellen.

She's alive and living the life she wants. She's cured. Be like her, Daryl."

Daryl looked at Ballarat and felt stupid for doubting him. The doctor was the only one on his side. It was now or never if he was going to live out the rest of his life in peace.

"Let them in," Daryl said.

Ballarat smiled.

"My pleasure."

The stretched walls ripped open, releasing a cloud of dust and the Beings.

* * *

Belinda ran to the side of the house and stopped at the bedroom windows. They were boarded up. She slid her fingers between the wood and the house and pulled. Some nails gave with ease, but some needed tugging. She took the board off and peaked into the room. It was old and deserted. With the handle of the gun, Belinda smashed the pane of glass. Through the hole, she saw the new bedroom from the past. Daryl and Tarallab were inside.

* * *

Daryl turned to the smashed window and saw Belinda crawl in from under the new curtain. Daryl pointed the shotgun at her; anger creased his face.

* * *

Belinda entered the room stuck in the past. Daryl pointed the shotgun at her. Dr. Tarallab stood next to him and smiled at her, enjoying himself. And behind them, the Beings who made their way through the walls. They did not look evil to Belinda, in fact, they looked like what Daryl drew before he was bitten, soft and angel-like.

"Welcome to the inside," Tarallab said to her. "Yes, that's them.

The infamous Beings."

"Leave," Daryl said to Belinda.

"Daryl, listen to me..." she began.

Someone banged on the bedroom door.

Daryl turned to it.

"If you're here, then who is that?" he asked.

"That must be her new boyfriend. Her fuck buddy," Tarallab offered.

Belinda flinched.

"What? That's your mother, Daryl," Belinda said.

"My mother?" Daryl asked. "No. Freddie's mother, isn't it?"

"I think it is your mother, Daryl. The one who deserted you when you were ten?" Tarallab asked. "The one that left you because you were a freak that saw these monsters in your sleep. She got rid of you, Daryl."

"Shut up," Belinda warned Tarallab, pointing her gun at him.

Tarallab smiled.

Belinda stepped towards the doctor. Daryl pulled the hammer back on the shotgun and pointed it at her. She quickly held her hands out in surrender, backing off.

Anger stretched in Daryl's face.

The pounding at the door grew louder.

Daryl pointed the gun at the door. He screamed, "Go away!"

Belinda yelled, "Tanya, move."

Daryl pulled the trigger.

* * *

Tanya stopped ramming the door and jumped back from it right before a hole blew out of the wood. She stepped back a few more feet and covered her gasping mouth with her hand, fearing the worst.

* * *

Daryl walked to Belinda. He wrung the shotgun in his hands as his face twisted in anger, anguish, and sweat.

"You're not going to hurt me anymore," Daryl whispered.

"I don't want to hurt you, sweetie."

"Shut up," Daryl exploded. "Don't call me that. You only use words like that when you love someone. You don't love me."

"How could you say that..."

"I heard you. You were fucking that guy. I called from the Clinic, and he picked up the phone, and I heard you talking...wanting him to cum on...you..."

Belinda looked at him.

"What Clinic, Daryl?"

Daryl laughed.

"The Ballarat Clinic. The hospital that I've been in for the last few months. The place you sent me to so that you could have an excuse to get rid of me."

"Daryl, listen, you were in a hospital in New York for only a week," Belinda stressed. "You were in a coma. You didn't go anywhere." Belinda moved closer, calming and careful, making Daryl's face soften. "There was no Ballarat Clinic. There was no other man. I was by your side all day, waiting for you to come back to me."

"Ask her about the abortion, Daryl," Tarallab said.

The anger rose back to Daryl's face.

"You're lying!" he screamed at her.

Daryl pushed her away with the length of the shotgun. Belinda's body slammed against the wall next to the closet.

"I'm not going to kill you, but if you get in my way, I will."

Belinda looked at Tarallab. The doctor smiled and winked at Belinda.

Daryl walked to the bed.

There was a little knock at the barricaded closet door next to her. "Help," said a little boy's voice from the other side.

* * *

Tanya pressed against the hall wall, tensing for another explosion of wood from the other side. The bedroom was quiet. She noticed a noise from the living room.

Tanya walked into the dark living room and heard a noise from the basement. It sounded like tapping, like a dog running on a hardwood floor and its nails slapping the surface. Tanya peered down the hole, but saw nothing.

"Ray," she called out.

There was a creaking in the kitchen.

The basement door push open. No one was there. As Tanya moved closer, she looked at the bottom of the basement door and saw a small army of baby creatures on four legs stumble out. They spotted Tanya.

"Shit," she whispered.

The army of little creatures ran for her.

* * *

At the bed, Daryl turned to Dr. Ballarat. The doctor held Daryl's face in his hands and smiled at him. He motioned with his head to the Beings waiting at the ripped walls.

"I'm ready," Daryl said.

Ballarat released Daryl and watched him lay on the bed with the shotgun in his hands. Daryl placed his back on the headboard and positioned the gun between his legs, pointing it at his head. He turned to the Beings. They moved closer, vicious and angry.

* * *

Belinda pushed the dresser away from the closet door, grabbing Tarallab's attention.

"Stop that," the doctor ordered.

Belinda ignored him and opened the closet door. She could not believe her eyes. The boy looked exactly like Freddie when he was ten. The little boy smiled and said, "Thank you."

She was speechless. Belinda watched the little boy run towards

Daryl.

Tarallab violently grabbed the little boy by the arm.

* * *

Tanya ran down the hall and entered Freddie's old bedroom. She closed the door and twisted the old lock on the knob. Tanya spotted a warped chair by the new desk and wedged it between the doorknob and the floor. Tanya backed away and drew her gun. Remembering that it was empty, Tanya dropped it to the floor.

The creatures started scratching on the other side of the door, trying to get in.

* * *

Daryl watched the Beings hover over his body, inches away. He kept his courage steady, pressing the barrel of the shotgun on his tongue and closing his eyes. He waited for the Beings to touch him.

* * *

Belinda ran up to Tarallab and tackled him, releasing the little boy from his grip. She landed on top of the doctor and pressed the revolver to his forehead.

"Leave him alone," she said.

The boy looked at her for a command. Belinda motioned with her head to Daryl, thinking that was whom the boy was running to. The boy continued towards Daryl.

Belinda turned back to Tarallab. His face rippled, distorting all the human kindness that rested in his skin. His eyes glowed an amber hue. The doctor's hand reached for Belinda's neck and squeezed. He then tossed her body off, sending her to the wall.

* * *

The bottom of the bedroom door chipped away, giving room for the baby creatures to slip in.

Tanya turned to the boarded window and, with an old globe sitting on the desk, smashed the glass. She continued to swing at the piece of wood nailed over the window, but the globe ended up receiving the most damage.

Tanya felt a claw dig into her leg, then another.

Tanya screamed.

* * *

Belinda fired at Tarallab as he turned to Freddie and Daryl. The bullets entered his back but did no harm to the doctor. He paid no mind to Belinda, focusing on Freddie. Belinda saw Tarallab reach out for the little boy but he missed him.

* * *

"Daryl!"

He opened his eyes. Looking around the Beings that floated centimeters away from him, Daryl saw Freddie standing by the bed.

"Open up," Freddie said.

Freddie jumped in the air and over the bed.

Daryl opened his arms to catch him.

The Beings moved out of Freddie's way.

* * *

Freddie's weight pressed to Daryl's body. Then the weight decreased. Keeping his eyes closed, Daryl felt Freddie soften, melting in his arms. But the boy didn't soak the mattress, he ran into Daryl's pores and entered his body. Daryl's soul exploded with warmth, with love, with remembrance.

* * *

Freddie slept in his parent's bed. He had such a good time with them that day that he did not want it to end. Mom and Dad were so happy and there was no weirdness with Dad. That was the best part. So he pretended to sleep in his bedroom and waited a half an hour. He then snuck out and made sure the coast was clear in the hall. He saw his Mom and Dad on the couch, watching television, holding each other. Happy. Freddie entered their dark bedroom. Knowing his way to the bed, he crawled in and made himself comfortable with his mother's pillow. He fell asleep. He woke up when he heard the bedroom door open. Fred remained quiet, wanting to surprise his father. He watched him go to the closet, turn the light on and off, and go to bed. Keeping the clothes he had on all day, his father stretched out on the bed and stuck his hands under the pillow. Dad didn't notice Freddie, so the boy remained still and waited for Mom. But she never came in. Freddie fell back asleep until a shifting on the bed woke him up. He turned around and saw his father sitting up with his back pressed against the headboard. Dad looked scared. Tears slid down his shaken face. Freddie immediately saw the revolver in his dad's hand and the bad end in his mouth. Freddie wanted to say something, anything to get the gun out of his father's mouth, but Freddie knew his father was in a state. He was sleepwalking and unreachable. Dad's body shivered. "Do it now, Daniel." Freddie looked across the room to see the owner of the voice. He was man in a sharp suit and very handsome. He stood in the dark room and walked over to the bed and said, "Do it for your son. Get better for him. Do it while you have the strength. Now." Freddie saw his father pull the trigger. There was a loud bang from the gun and a dull squish from the back of his father's head hitting the wall. The handsome man laughed triumphantly. He looked at Freddie and said, "I'll see you later." The man faded into the darkness. Freddie turned back to his dead father. The boy felt numb and cold. He tried to shake his father back to life but it was no good. He heard his Mom call his father's name.

Freddie panicked and ran off the bed. He went to the closet and hid there. He kept the door open, staring at his father, hoping he would get up and move, staring harder and harder...then a woman entered the room and cried. She turned to Freddie. She seemed to know him. Freddie noticed a man on the bed with a bloody head. Freddie had no idea who the man was. He then forgot himself.

* * *

Daryl opened his eyes. His head hurt from the rush of memories. The Beings floated around him, waiting with their claws ready. He saw Belinda by the closet door, staring at him. Ballarat expectantly waited by the bed.

"You killed my father," Daryl stated. He lowered the shotgun from his head.

Ballarat smiled and said, "No. You saw it."

"I saw you. You tricked him. It was all crap. Final Phase? It was all a...fuckin' trick."

"Well, then, what are you going to do, Daryl? Go home? Go ahead. Leave. Go home, because it will never end. They will continue to haunt you. If you don't do it now, you will eventually do it."

"He's right, Daryl," Belinda offered.

Ballarat motioned to her, stressing his point.

"They will never leave you. They love you. He poisoned you to see them the way they are now. He's making you see them as demons," Belinda said.

Ballarat turned to her. His skull throbbed in anger. "Shut up." He turned to Daryl. "Don't listen to her."

"Look at him, Daryl. He knows I'm right. He's scared. If you let them embrace you, they'll show their true selves to you."

Daryl studied Ballarat. He saw the nervousness under his sharp features. The doctor's jaw shifted, waiting for a death sentence.

Belinda moved past the doctor and kneeled down in front of the bed.

"Remember the bite. Everyone in your family had the same bite. The Beings didn't turn bad until after the bite," Belinda said. "He poisoned you, Daryl. He poisoned them all and tricked them into killing themselves."

Daryl remembered the question: Look at how great it is. How could that turn bad?

* * *

"Influence," Daryl whispered.

Belinda had no idea what he meant by that, but she knew it was a good sign. She reached out and grabbed the shotgun. With wet eyes, Daryl looked at her.

"I'm sorry," Daryl said. "I'm so sorry. I love you."

"I love you, too. Our baby loves you."

Daryl released a sob.

"Our baby," he said. "It's really alive?"

"Of course."

"It was all in my head," Daryl whispered.

Belinda stepped away with the shotgun.

Daryl turned to the Beings hovering around him. He touched one of their vile faces. His fingers moved past the ugliness as if it was sludge and pressed a smooth, waxy surface. The demonic features faded away and the peaceful, child-like features came forth. The Being moved its hand to Daryl's cheek and wiped a tear away.

Daryl opened his arms to them.

* * *

The army of baby creatures covered Tanya. She squirmed, screamed, and fought. She grabbed one off her body and threw it away, but they just came back, biting and clawing.

Tanya felt like giving up and succumbing to their violence. She wanted to die.

* * *

The Beings hugged Daryl. His arms wrapped around three of them while two hugged his legs. Belinda noticed his bitten hand sticking out, pressing to a Being's back. The bite wound spurted an amber liquid. The puckered skin on the wound closed up once the last drop of amber puked out.

Daryl's face peaked out from between the Beings. He was happy, truly happy like he used to on the videotape that Kate recorded.

Belinda cried weak with joy.

* * *

Daryl noticed the Beings moving off his body. They turned to Ballarat. The doctor pressed against the wall and smiled, trying so hard to keep his cool, hiding his fear.

"This isn't over. I'll be back for the two in your belly," Ballarat said. "They'll eventually call me like you did, Daryl. They always call for me."

The Beings floated for Ballarat. They took the doctor in their arms and hugged him tight. He screamed out as a bright yellow and green light exploded from his body and filled the room.

Daryl, blinded, moved off the bed and searched for Belinda. She went into his arms. They held each other in the Being's light and Ballarat's screams.

* * *

Suddenly, they stopped. The baby creatures' mouths and claws released her and their bodies went limp. Tanya shook them off and crawled away.

* * *

Belinda woke up in Daryl's arms. They were on the floor. Daryl slept. She looked around the room. It was old and run down. The Beings and Tarallab were gone. Belinda felt like she had lost time. The last thing she remembered was the light and the screams. Belinda had no idea how she ended up with Daryl on the floor.

Daryl woke up with sleepy eyes and looked at her. Belinda propped herself up on an elbow and smiled at him.

"Hey, sleepyhead," she said.

"I feel like I slept a thousand years," Daryl said.

"You did," Belinda responded. "Do you remember anything?"

"I remember everything."

"Are you alright?"

Daryl took her cheek in his hand and moved her head closer to his. He breathed in her scent and said, "I am now."

* * *

Tanya had no idea what just happened. The army of baby creatures was dead. On bitten and scratched legs, she stepped around them and made her way to the hall. Tanya walked outside and saw Belinda and Freddie, a grown man also known as Daryl, leave the master bedroom. Tanya stared, speechless.

Freddie looked back at her and casually said, "Mom?"

Tanya released a sob.

"Oh, shit. Thank you, God," Tanya said.

Tanya ran to him. Freddie took her in his arms. "I'm so sorry," Tanya said.

Freddie held her close. "It's okay. It's okay, Mom."

* * *

Belinda left Daryl and Tanya alone in the hall. She walked into the living room, and wondered what happened to Ray. She went into the flooded kitchen, around the exploded creature, and stepped through the door that led to the basement. Belinda carefully moved down the weak stairs and into the basement.

Belinda moved through the maze of boxes, calling out Ray's name. There was no response, and she saw why. Ray was on the floor. Little bites and deep scratches covered his body. Next to him was the torn carcass of a four-legged creature. She figured that he killed the creature, but the babies from the belly ended up killing him.

Belinda kneeled down next to his body and pressed her fingertips to Ray's open eyelids. She closed them. Belinda filled with guilt and started to cry.

"Thank you," she whispered.

* * *

Tanya looked around her New York apartment and made sure everything was clean. It was. In fact, it had been clean all day, but she was nervous. She wanted to make a good impression on her two new guests. Freddie – she couldn't get used to calling him Daryl - kept reminding her all week that her new guests were only one month old and that the appearance of the apartment wasn't going to matter to them. Tanya didn't believe him.

They were expected in five minutes. Tanya sat on the couch and waited.

Tanya moved into the apartment one month after Freddie regained his memory on Tunisia Ave. When she took them back to the house that night to clean up, Freddie made a comment about the house: the place reeked of Ballarat. Tanya agreed. Freddie helped her find an apartment, actually, more like a condominium. Tanya said she couldn't afford it on her salary, but Freddie told her not to worry. He would take care of it.

Before that, they buried Ray. Tanya felt guilty about his death. He killed two of those huge creatures to save Freddie, only to be ripped apart by those little baby creatures. They showed their appreciation by purchasing a huge tombstone, matching the new stone they bought for Danny.

The police investigated the happening at 256 Tunisia Ave. They kept it quiet due to the strange carcasses that were found in the house.

There was no question of who murdered Ray; it was obvious to the coroner. Besides that there was no crime, but there were a lot of questions involving Freddie. He told the investigators realistic parts of the truth. Freddie woke up from his coma and remembered where he lived as a child. He went home.

Specialists in the occult and in biology called them from time to time, wanting to get their thoughts on the creatures in the house. They avoided the calls, letting the specialists figure out where the four-legged creatures came from.

Freddie and Belinda went back to New York. Freddie and Belinda saw their doctor, Belinda especially. They were both in perfect health. The baby was fine.

Life ran quietly for 8 months. Freddie went on a small tour for his new Michelina book, which peaked at the bottom of the Bestseller's, and that was fine with Daryl. It did not affect the network from going through with the Saturday morning cartoon. Freddie accepted their offer.

Belinda postponed her tour and agreed to do some tri-state shows a few months after the birth, some videos, and a lot of press.

Then the birth happened. Belinda had twins, a boy and a girl. Everyone did extra flips. It was the perfect reward.

As for the Beings, they came back, and Freddie continued to sleepwalk with them. It was all good and harmless.

The door bell rang.

Tanya stood up, looked around the room, and then walked to the door.

"Who is it?" she called out, kidding around.

"Ah, jeez, ma. Would you let us in? These two are heavy," Freddie whined.

"Shut up, Daryl," Belinda shot back.

"Owe," Freddie said. "I was just kidding."

Tanya smiled and opened the door. There they were. Daniel Raymond Hersh and Kathleen Hersh, gurgling and dribbling with joy.